William Pett Ridge

The Second Opportunity of Mr. Staplehurst

A novel

William Pett Ridge

The Second Opportunity of Mr. Staplehurst
A novel

ISBN/EAN: 9783337027285

Printed in Europe, USA, Canada, Australia, Japan

Cover: Foto ©Andreas Hilbeck / pixelio.de

More available books at **www.hansebooks.com**

THE SECOND OPPORTUNITY

OF

MR. STAPLEHURST

𝔄 𝔑ovel

By W. PETT RIDGE

AUTHOR OF "A CLEVER WIFE"

NEW YORK

HARPER & BROTHERS PUBLISHERS

1896

THE SECOND OPPORTUNITY OF

MR. STAPLEHURST

THE SECOND OPPORTUNITY OF
MR. STAPLEHURST

CHAPTER I

THE Nomadic Club was holding its monthly dinner, and the dinner had reached that happy moment when dessert arrives. Quite one-half of the men in this world look upon the eating of a long dinner as a tiresome crime, and nearly every-body at the four long tables was content to see nuts on the table. The Nomadic Club had no home (which was right and appropriate on the part of Nomads); it existed only for the purpose of dining once a month.

To this feast it was its cunning habit to invite as guest of the club the most prominent man it could catch, and extort from this guest a speech.

"Members of the Nomadic Club, you may smoke!"

The members edged their chairs slightly back

from the tables, and cigars and cigarettes and pipes came out. The youngest members smoked pipes under the impression that it made them look Bohemian.

"Look here, Staplehurst," whispered the Chair, "I'll propose the Queen first, and then , after a bit I'll propose your health, and then——"

"My dear fellow," said the Guest of the Evening, with much fervor, "if I have any influence with the gods, some happy accident will intervene to prevent you. I rather fancy a thunderbolt will come through the ceiling and knock you over, but I'm not sure about the details. I had no idea that a speech was indispensable."

"For a man who has written the big book of the year," said the Chair, "you are an unconscionably stupid person, Staplehurst. Why, this ought to be the proudest moment of your life! If any one thing represents Fame, this does. Here are you, invited by a body of representative men in art and literature and what not——"

"What not is good."

"And yet you aren't happy. Why, upon my word, Staplehurst—do you want a light?—upon my word, I believe you're one of the men who don't know when they're really well off."

Gilbert Staplehurst looked at the red end of his cigar and stroked his short-clipped beard thoughtfully.

"I am nearly always crying for the moon," he confessed. "It's rather pleasant to desire the absolutely unattainable."

"*Soyez content, mon ami.* You have a charming wife."

"That's quite true," agreed Gilbert Staplehurst with much heartiness.

"You're earning goodness knows how much a year out of your books."

"My income is pretty fair, certainly."

"Big house at Chelsea; no children to bother you; only slightly gray; not corpulent as to figure. Why, bless my soul, Staplehurst, what more do you want?"

The Chair, rising to propose the loyal toast, looked down indignantly at his friend. Chair was so perturbed that he threw a suggestion of defiance into his brief proposal of the health of Her Majesty that was scarcely necessary.

"Now," said Chair, resuming his seat—"now I'm going to propose your health directly, Staplehurst. You'd better make a note or two of what you want to say in reply."

The man on the other side of Staplehurst nudged him, and he turned.

"When are you coming up to my studio?"

"I think I'll come soon, MacManus. Mrs. Staplehurst is going away for six weeks, taking her mother to the Cape, and I'm to be a bachelor."

"Ay, man," said Mr. MacManus, "some of you get all the luck."

"It will be rather miserable for me," said Staplehurst thoughtfully. "We're neither of us very happy when we're apart."

"Ye're a bit old to be in love, man. The coortin' days are by, surely!"

"I think a man should always be his wife's sweetheart."

"It depends," said Mr. MacManus thoughtfully—"it depends to a great extent on the wife. In streect confidence, I'll tell you, now, that Mrs. MacManus will never toolerate for a single moment any thing of the kind. Thirty years ago, now, it was so deeferent: I was a bit lad then, and I married her, and ay," MacManus sighed, "we were happy."

Gilbert Staplehurst nodded his head in acquiescence.

"There's nothing so precious," he said, "as youth."

He wrote on the back of the *menu* with a small pencil three words—"Thanks," "Success," "Youth." The word "youth" he underlined, that he might not forget to speak of the topic of which the word was to remind him. As he held his pencil on the card, he looked before him. For a moment he saw, not four long white-clothed tables with quick-eyed men seated thereat, but a train coming in at Paddington, and a youth alighting before the train stopped, in his impatience to make a name for himself with the least possible delay—a well-looking youth, with plenty of wavy hair; with the complexion that health brings, and the quick step that comes with twenty-two and thinks of going at forty and fifty years. The youth of twenty-two looks about him delightedly, observing every thing, almost laughing with the sheer joy of living. He has been up from Devonshire three times before, but always with an economic aunt or a careful uncle. This morning he is alone. To-day the fight begins. He, young Gilbert Staplehurst, is his own regiment ; he has no one at his back to encourage him. Outside Paddington Station——

"Fellow-members of the Nomadic Club" (Mr. Gilbert Staplehurst, as he hears the Chair's voice, swiftly comes down from the clouds of retrospection to the table-land of reality), "I have to ask you to drink with me the health of the guest of the evening, Mr. Gilbert Staplehurst [Cheers]. We are not accustomed at our dinners to use the language that flatters at the expense of the language that is true, and it is only right that I should tell you frankly that Mr. Staplehurst, unlike ourselves, has his faults [Laughter] ; he has the impudence not to be satisfied with his career, albeit that career has been one that nearly all of us present here to-night envy [Hear, hear !].

"I need not give you a list of the works which have made the name of Gilbert Staplehurst famous wherever English literature is read. I need not tell you how, after some years of steady toil and, as Stevenson puts it, 'of slogging away, day in and day out,' he not so very long ago found himself one of the few men whom the world delights to honor [Cheers]. We of the Nomadic Club, who desire to meet talent and acknowledge its existence, have done ourselves

the pleasure of asking him to be our guest to-
night, in order that we may assure him of our
regard [Hear, hear!], of our admiration [Hear,
hear!], and our sincere felicitations [Cheers]. I
give you the health of Gilbert Staplehurst; and
if one or two of you can sing without causing any
fatality [A laugh], we might give it with musical
honors" [Cheers].

The Nomadic Club was made up of excellent
young men, most earnest in their various profes-
sions, and with many public and private virtues;
but of these virtues accuracy in music was not
one. Nevertheless, the congratulatory chorus of
"For he's a jolly good fellow" was given with
great enthusiasm; and if some did sing an octave
lower than others, their hearts were doubtless in
the right place. Something came to the throat
of Mr. Staplehurst as, alone seated, he watched
the excitement. A good proportion of the members were on what is called the right side of
thirty; some were as absurdly young as twenty-
one. The noise they were making delighted these
younger ones, and they gave the "Hip-hip-
hurrah!" with so much of strenuousness that a
jovial smoking-concert in the hall below, finding
itself outnoised, sent up presently a polite mes-

sage by the waiter to enquire whether the earth-quake was over.

"It's very good of you to say those pleasant things," said Gilbert Staplehurst.

"Did it rather neatly, didn't I?" said the Chair humorously. "I suppose that Demosthenes and myself are really the only two orators worth mentioning."

"I am quite serious," said the Guest of the Evening.

"You shouldn't be, Staplehurst. Life is not a performance to be serious about. The best way is to look on and laugh."

"I should laugh," said Staplehurst good-temperedly, "if I were only as young as some of these lads round me. It's a fine thing to have the world before you, instead of behind."

"No use worrying about that," said the Chair wisely; "it can't be altered. The whole scheme of things is not to be changed to suit even distinguished writers. My own opinion is that the gods know what they're about, and that it's all for the——"

The secretary of the Club came and whispered to the Chair.

"Certainly, Rowlands; let him sing now by

all means if he wants to get away. Mr. Staplehurst can reply afterward."

The piano in the corner of the large room was
moved to a new position, and its candles were
lighted. A tall youth finished his coffee, and
strolled with an air of elaborate negligence from
his seat to the music-stool. Then, in a most
excellent baritone voice, and to his own vamped
accompaniments, he sang:

"There are joys of this earth of most excellent worth,.
  That to most of us sometimes arrive ;
  But there's one that is sweeter than others you meet here—
  'Tis the joy just of being alive.
  For when——"

"Will you have a Chartreuse or something,
Staplehurst?" asked the Chair.

"No, thank you—not before I've got over this
speech business."

"Cheer up," said the Chair encouragingly.

"'At such a time,'" quoted Gilbert Staplehurst, with a laugh, "'the mind, Mr. Wilfer,
naturally reverts to the past.'"

"You men with a past are nearly as great
'a nuisance as men with a future. What's the
matter with your past?"

"Nothing," exclaimed Staplehurst definitely.

He glanced at the long white ash of his cigar. "Nothing at all. Twenty years ago was the happiest time of my life."

"Nonsense!"

"I am speaking," said the Guest of the Evening, with much earnestness—"I am speaking the absolute truth."

"That's a habit that will grow on you, if you're not careful," remarked the Chair warningly.

The baritone youth at the piano concluded his song with a triumphant manner:

> " And here's to the health and the wisdom and wealth
> Of the man who is always alive!"

And hurried off.

"Now, Staplehurst."

Tremendous applause. Clattering of knives, tapping of tables, the confused "hear, hear"-ing that reporters called "cheers."

The tall figure of the Guest stood up. He looked around the room at the flushed faces of his young hosts; he passed his hand over his prematurely grayish hair, and looked down at the notes before him—"Thanks."

"Gentlemen: let me try to tell you, if I can,

how much I appreciate the compliment that you are paying me to-night. The good feeling of one's fellow-workers is a priceless possession; you, by your kindness to-night, are making me believe that my enemies are few, and that my friends are many [Cheers]. I shall not forget this evening. It is not every thing in this life that happens precisely as one would wish, and the fault is perhaps generally one's own. I often think that, if we were permitted to live our lives over again, we might profit from the experience of the first essay [Laughter], and comport ourselves with something more of discretion. But under the present rules of the game it is not permitted to have a second innings, and we have to take our own life as we find it, and do the best we can with the brief training that we get. I should like, though, to think that whatever may happen to me after I leave this room nothing may erase from my mind the memory of this evening with you all " [Loud cheers].

Gilbert Staplehurst looked down at the second word on his notes, "Success."

"Your chairman, gentlemen, has been kind enough to refer to one or two of my books which have attained some circulation. The worst form of conceit is the assumption of self-contempt, and I wish to declare frankly that it gives me great pleasure to hear my work praised [Hear, hear !]. I passed through years of good, solid, hard work, as some of you perhaps have done [Hear, hear !], as some of you perhaps are doing [Cheers], before I found that the age beamed upon me. I don't regret that apprenticeship. I am sincere in saying, gentlemen, that those were the happiest, the most delightful days of my life [A laugh]. I am sorry to hear a laugh. I can assure you that I am speaking sincerely."

The Club cheered, and the gloomy, straight-haired youth who had ejaculated the Mephistopheles-like laugh was frowned at by his neighbors and became a prey to gloom.

" To be young, to have youth on your side, that is the true secret of happiness. Your future is in your own hands then ; you can make it, mar it, or play the fool with it, just as you please. We—and when I say we, I am holding a brief for the middle-aged folk—we, I say, were all young once. I feel to-night that I wish it were permitted to be young twice [Laughter]. What mistakes one might omit, what waste of time one might avoid, how quickly one might reach the goal of happiness ! I'm afraid, gentlemen, that it is useless to argue the question, or even to submit here to the gods the inconvenience of the present arrangement [Laughter]. All that we can do, all that I can recommend you to do is to

" ' Gather ye rosebuds while ye may,'

and do your best while youth is with you, for you will never have a second opportunity.

"Gentlemen, only one word more."

One or two youths sighed at hearing this remark. They knew that, with average orators, this phrase usually precedes a lengthy harangue.

"One word more. That word shall be of thanks to you, of thanks to the British public, of thanks to my dear wife, whom I shall see this evening before she leaves on a trip to the Cape, and who has always been my best and dearest friend [Cheers], and, finally, God bless you all!"

Staplehurst closed his speech hurriedly because his reference to Mrs. Staplehurst had just for the moment made him feel as though he could not trust his voice. The room cheered and rattled glasses, and when a flushed young journalist rose and cried "Good old G.," the room cheered again the familiar initial.

"Now, if it won't appear rude," said Staplehurst to the Chair, "I should like to hear one more song and then slip off. They won't mind, will they? Mrs. Staplehurst has to go by the nine-thirty train from Paddington to her mother's house, and they go away by the early mail to Southampton to-morrow morning. She's a very good old lady, the mother."

"*Do* be careful, Staplehurst," said the Chair protestingly; "you seem bent on upsetting all the traditions that have made England noble. A man who will say a good word for his wife's mother is a man who will say any thing !"

"Nevertheless it is the truth."

"That is no excuse. Besides, you are not the man to stand up for truth. Fiction has always been your best friend."

"If I were beginning my life again, I wonder whether I should choose literature ?"

"A man," interposed MacManus from the other side, "never chooses his path in life. The path just chooses him."

"I'm not quite sure that I understand what that means," remarked the Chair. "I'm going to call on Waterson for a recitation."

Gilbert Staplehurst waited for this. It was a powerful recitation of the Kipling order.

"He's a gruntin', grizzly fool with a head just like a mule,
But he's just the man to fight the Widow's fight ;
And when——"

The Nomadic Club cheered at the end with sufficient turmoil to permit the guest of the evening to shake hands unobserved with a few of his immediate friends; to walk down stairs for his hat and coat,—a touch of rheumatism in the left shoulder made him wince as the cloak-room man helped him with his long overcoat,—and to take hansom for home.

"Right you are, sir. Winder up or dahn ?"

"Up," said Mr. Staplehurst; "the night's chilly."

"Ah," said the cabman sympathetically through the trap, "we can't stand the 'eat, sir, and we can't stand the cold, sir, like what we used to in our young days."

"What the devil do you mean by that? " asked Staplehurst sharply.

"What do I mean, sir?" repeated the cabman. "What do I mean ? Why, I don't mean no offence, that's a very sure thing."

"No, no; of course not!"

Staplehurst felt ashamed of his sudden out-
burst. He stepped into the hansom. "Paddington Station."

"I dunno how it is," muttered the cabman to
himself, "but I never seem ible to say the right
thing some'ow. Lord knows I try to be nice,
too. Whoever would 'a' guessed that he'd got so
ror all in a moment just because I sympathized
with him."

The hansom went swiftly Bayswater way.
Staplehurst, looking out through the window of
the cab, found his mind bent on the consideration, not of to-night's dinner, not of the cheers
of the Nomadic Club, not of the kind things said
by every one about himself and his work, not of
the position that to-night's event marked as it
were in scarlet letters; instead his mind persistently centred itself on the incidents of twenty-
five years ago. The scent came from the trees
in the park, with it a suggestion of wallflowers:
outside the railings the dilapidated artist held
his evening exhibition of art with the aid of
candles stuck in gingerbeer bottles.

Suddenly came one of those amazing little
scenes that keep London streets from being

commonplace. Three youths, long-legged, bare-
headed, and dank-haired, in blue pants and vest
and running shoes and nothing else, came madly
down Edgware Road, racing for some goal with
a determination that made them oblivious of
the ironical cheers of small boys on the pavement.

"Go it! Go *it!* Why don't you run?"

"'Urry along, there; 'urry along! You'll be
late 'ome, if you ain't careful."

"I say, mister, where's your hat? You've bin
and lost it, I lay."

The odd sight somehow assisted Mr. Staplehurst's reminiscences. He had been an athletic
enthusiast in his youth, and now, whenever he
had to see Dr. Ripon of Wimpole Street, Ripon
always told him that he was paying for the
over-training in his youth. These wise men of
Wimpole Street are ever giving one unavailing
information in regard to first causes. Staplehurst, too, like every one else of his age,
had to use an increased discretion in regard
to solids that are eaten and liquids that are
drunk.

"At twenty," said Staplehurst, looking at a
restaurant—"at twenty I used to be able to

eat nearly every thing. I wonder why some pleasures are not reserved for the later life. Why," said Mr. Staplehurst expostulatingly to the cab horse—"why cram them all into the early years? Ay?"

The cab horse seemed quite ignorant of the answer to the riddle.

"From twenty to thirty, or a little after, all the joy comes; all the excitement of a man's life. He falls in love, he falls out; he makes the foundation of his career, and sees that the corner-stone is well and truly laid; he——"

"Hi!"

The cab pulled up. A youthful couple had hailed it with so much decision that the cabman did not dare but obey.

"Dear Mr. Staplehurst!" It was the youth who spoke. "Madge and I are just getting home, and we caught sight of you. You don't mind our stopping you?"

"It's dreadfully rude, I am afraid," said the young lady; "but we're so happy that we are doing all sorts of mad things."

Mr. Staplehurst stepped carefully out of the hansom and shook hands.

"And when did you come back from your honeymoon, young people?" he asked genially.

"Only on Saturday. And we've had the most delightful tour you can possibly——"

"Of course you have. And you liked Italy? Did it behave well to you?"

"Italy conducted itself charmingly," said the beaming young lady. "In fact, all Europe conspired on our behalf. And Herbert found, on his return, such excellent news."

"Had a letter from old Purfleet," said the young husband, taking up his part in the duet, "offering me——"

He whispered confidentially.

"Good!" cried Gilbert Staplehurst. "I congratulate you. And I wish you once more all sorts of good luck. You have every thing in your favor."

"We are going to settle down," she declared with enthusiasm, "into the quietest young couple you ever invented, Mr. Staplehurst. Do you remember Mr. and Mrs. Warburgh in that last novel of yours?"

"I had the inestimable pleasure of reading that delightful work," said Staplehurst, "and——"

"We are going to take them as our model, aren't we, dear?"

"The sweet girl lets her tongue run on, sir," said the young fellow apologetically, "and forgets that we are keeping you here in the cold. How's the sciatica, sir?"

"Don't talk about it," said Mr. Staplehurst. "I pretend to ignore it as long as I can. Good-by, lucky young children."

"Good-by. Give our love to dear Mrs. Staplehurst. Good-by."

Gilbert Staplehurst stood on the pavement and watched the two young people hurry along in the direction of the Marble Arch. The lady with one hand bunched up her skirts carefully, as young matrons (with an eye to dress bills) do; with the other she took affectionately the arm of her joyful husband.

Staplehurst sighed and turned to walk.

"'Ere!" expostulated the cabman. "'Arf a minute, sir; 'arf a minute! How do you think a poor kebby's going to get drink and smoke and food if respectable middle-aged gents go bilking of him like this? If you don't want to be drove all the w'y to Paddington, why——"

It dawned upon Staplehurst that in his absence

of mind he had forgotten his cab. He tossed, as peace-offering, a four-shilling piece to the indignant cabman and stepped in.

"Good luck to you, sir!" cried the cabman, with a quick change of manner. "May you never know what it is to——"

"Drive on!" said Mr. Staplehurst.

CHAPTER II

Paddington Station was, as to one part, in a state of serenity and partial darkness; as to platform No. 1 it was bustle, activity, and light. A few passengers, nervous of being left behind, were seated in the train, and in order to get well forward with the work of saying farewell, had already kissed their friends several times over. In the refreshment room men were swallowing cups of coffee and trying (with no success) to make the reserved young ladies who had served them to smile.

At the big bookstall, passengers read the titles of a lot of books with an air of acute criticism, finally rejecting all of them in favor of an evening newspaper with a full account of the last and best and brightest murder. A blustering commercial traveller, annoyed at being charged the correct amount for his excess luggage, used language to the calm porter of such a character that a small, fat, white baby near, of Puritanical views, wailed aloud and absolutely refused to be com-

forted until the commercial gent cooled down
and resumed the language to which the small
baby had been accustomed.

Mr. Gilbert Staplehurst entered the station
and went in search of his wife. Her good-looking face lighted up as she saw him.

"I am so glad you are in time to see me off,
dear. You're not tired out with the evening?"

"I am just a little fatigued," said Mr. Staplehurst. He stood on the platform with his wife;
the guard touched his cap and locked up a
compartment.

"They were all very enthusiastic and noisy
and——"

"And your head aches a little?" Mrs. Staplehurst passed her small plump hand over his
forehead with an affectionate action. "I wish I
were not going now. Only poor mother will
expect me and——"

"My dear," said Staplehurst, holding her
chin, "you must think of somebody besides your
husband."

"My mother and my husband are the only
folk I want to think of. I'm only a woman."

They walked toward the bookstall. The big,
broad platform was busy, and passengers with

mountains of luggage were becoming scarlet with worry.

"And," Mrs. Staplehurst laughed nervously, "because I'm only a woman——"

"It's enough, dear."

"Only a woman, I can't help a very stupid feeling that something extraordinary is going to happen before I return."

"If you will give me a hint, Alice, I will see what can be done. Would you like——"

"I almost wish, Gilbert, that you too were coming for a change."

"If I am bored with my own company I *will* go somewhere."

"I shall write as often as possible," went on Mrs. Staplehurst, taking up two or three periodicals, "and—I have a two-shilling piece, dear—and if you can find time, you must send me just a line to Madeira to meet us on our return. That's the only chance you will have. The doctor says that dear mother must keep going."

"If anything happens, dear, to prevent you from getting a note you mustn't think that I have forgotten you."

She pressed his arm, and Mr. Staplehurst laughed suddenly.

"Upon my word, Alice," he whispered, "we're talking as though we were only half our real age. Nobody who heard us would imagine that we had been married for twenty-five years!"

"I don't believe it is twenty-five years," declared Mrs. Staplehurst obstinately. "I believe it has been more like twenty-five minutes. Is that the bell for my train? Perhaps I had better take my seat."

The guard was there. Guard anxious to have a word or two to say to Mr. Staplehurst, in order that he might quote the author's responses in Exeter, where Staplehurst's popularity was great. To-morrow, in the Northcote Arms, guard would repeat word for word his brief talk with the West Country novelist, and listeners would urge cider upon the guard as recompense.

"You'll look after Mrs. Staplehurst, guard?"

"Don't you fear about that, sir. How far's her going?"

"Just to Torquay."

"Nothin' shall 'appen to your good lady this side Exeter, sir. Yew're not going?"

The guard turned his lamp on Staplehurst's evening dress and noted one or two details for the information of the Northcote Arms.

"No, Barker. I'm to be left alone for six weeks or more. I sha'n't know what to make of it at first."

"And the baby, Barker?" interposed Mrs. Staplehurst from the carriage—"the last one, I mean?"

"He's a fine child, ma'am," said Mr. Barker, "a fine child, if ever there was one. But I tell the missis that it mun stop now. Ten children in a family is a good mod'rate number. May I shut the door, ma'am? Thank you, sir, thank you. My eldest boy read your last book, sir."

"Is he still alive, Barker?"

"Bless you, sir, he roared over some parts of it—fairly roared, he did. And then other parts made him look very straight."

Mr. Staplehurst smiled at the compliment. It is a hard literary heart that does not rejoice when the compliment unexpected arrives. Barker, lamp in hand, ran forward; the inspector appealed to passengers to take their seats, and begged non-passengers to stand away from the train. To the railway official the world is ever a reformatory school of undisciplined pupils.

"No other message, dear?"

"No," said Mrs. Staplehurst.

The tears were in her eyes, for some women will weep even at the most affecting moments.

"Excepting to kiss you."

Staplehurst put his head in at the window and kissed his wife. The train jerked; a newspaper boy played lawn tennis with evening journals, his server using coppers; the guard stepped into his brake and shouted something satirical to a lamp-man about the lampman's face; Gilbert Staplehurst took off his hat and stood bareheaded as the train drew out.

Then he went outside and stepped again into his cab.

"Cheyne Gardens," said Mr. Staplehurst shortly.

It must have been the parting from his dear wife that made the fare thoughtful. He leaned over the splash-board and looked at the lighted shops, at the crowds on the pavement, at tall, lanky scarlet soldiers escorting dwarf-like servants, and all the ordinary sights of the streets —he looked at these without seeing them. He could only see a delighted young couple, in the hats of years ago, walking in Kensington Gardens and telling each other——

"Here you are, cabman."

Mr. Staplehurst thrust his hand up to stop the cab.

"Will this do for you, cabman?"

"Sir," said the cabman, with a burst of enthusiasm, "you're what I call a gentleman. You know how to treat a poor kebby, you do. You've got a 'eart as——"

"Good-night."

On the narrow table in the hall was a letter marked, "By hand. Immediate." Mr. Staplehurst took it upstairs to his comfortable study, switched on the electric light, and took a cigarette. They were of a very mild brand; he did not dare to smoke much. With a small paper-cutter he opened the envelope.

"Hang it!" exclaimed Mr. Staplehurst.

The editor of a weekly review begged that his dear friend Staplehurst would let him have, by ten o'clock on the following morning, without fail, a two-thousand-word article in continuation of a series of light mythological studies that had appeared before. The editor hoped that his dear friend Staplehurst would not disappoint him. The editor had (he said) tons of ordinary stuff; what he wanted, and what was so difficult to get, was the stuff extraordinary. Editor suggested Juno as a possible subject. Ten o'clock to-morrow morning.

Mr. Staplehurst pressed the knob by the mantel-piece.

" Martha! "

" Yes, sir. Did you ring, sir ? ".

"You servants needn't stay up. I shall be at work for a while. And, by the bye, I may be going away. I'm not sure, yet, but it is possible. If I do go, you can manage, I suppose ? "

Martha was a middle-aged maid who had been with the Staplehursts for years.

" I *think* I know how to manage, sir," she said severely.

"Yes, yes, of course ! Those men haven't been about the telephone, I suppose ? "

" Why, yes, sir. Haven't you noticed it ? Here it is, in the corner of the room, just where you said it was to be put."

"I hadn't noticed it." Staplehurst rose and went toward the newly fixed instrument. It was a neat little affair; he had ordered that it should be furnished with all the latest im' provements.

"Wonderful thing, sir, steam—I mean to say 'lectricity," remarked Martha. " I'm told that you can talk to almost any body and anywheres through these."

"Almost," said Mr. Staplehurst.

He took the tubes off their supports and peered curiously at the wires.

"I wonder," said Martha, "what in the world they'll be inventing of next. Reely, there don't seem any bounds to what they can do nowadays, does there, sir? Once they set their mind on a thing, why, it's as good as done. At least," added Martha respectfully, "that's how it seems to me. There must be a limit to it all some day. Some day some one 'll go a bit too far and then——"

Martha stopped because she felt that she was becoming too talkative.

"Good-night, sir."

"Good-night, Martha. You won't forget what I said?"

"*I* sha'n't forget, sir."

The article took about an hour and a half to write. Staplehurst, reading it through, felt bound to smile here and there, tired as he was. The defence of Juno was definite and uncompromising; the article argued quaintly that she and Jove were really model characters with no thought of guile, that their characters had been besmirched by the ancient society journals thirsting for scandal in high places.

"It is to be regretted that so long a time should have been allowed to elapse before a proper investigation into these affairs was made. It is indeed a crying scandal to our ancestors whose

> " ' swords are rust,
> Their bodies dust,
> Their souls are with the saints, we trust,'

that they never moved hand or foot to defend the character of the much-traduced Juno.

"For the Victorian Era this has been reserved. The present writer, although he has only in this brief paper essayed to point the way, trusts that the Government will lose no time in offering a Commission of the House for search after accuracy in these matters. Commissions have been held on subjects less tangible; on none more fraught with interest to the community."

"Why, bless my soul," said Mr. Staplehurst, as he enclosed the scrip and marked it for delivery by an express messenger, "it was over a mythological article that I earned my first money. I can remember how my heart jumped then; I never have that delight now. I believe that I was happier then in my dullest moments than I am now in my brightest."

He walked to the telephone and looked down on the small mahogany board.

"I wish," he said wearily—"I wish to goodness I were young again."

A ring at the telephone, one distinct ring. Mr. Staplehurst was so astonished that he did not at first answer it.

Another ring. Loud, insistent, complaining! Mr. Staplehurst took the tubes from off their supports and placed them to his ears.

"Hullo there!" he cried.

"Oh, you've answered at last, have you? Are you Gilbert Staplehurst?"

"Yes, yes, of course I am. Who are you? Speak up, please. Don't mumble so. Speak out distinctly."

"I can speak distinctly enough," said the voice at the other end testily, "if you'd only listen. You people fly into such a temper over the smallest——"

"I'm not in a temper," exclaimed Mr. Staplehurst warmly, "I was never calmer in my life. It's *you* who are behaving stupidly. If you will kindly keep cool, and tell me what you want——"

"I don't want any thing. I've got every thing I want."

"You're lucky," said Mr. Staplehurst.

"I know that. It's my special department. But look here! I mustn't bandy words with you. I have a good many things to look after, and I can't afford to waste a whole night over one individual."

Gilbert Staplehurst bit his lips to avoid an excursion into intemperate language. There is no more trying situation in this world than to have to deal through the telephone with a defiant unknown.

"Will you allow me to speak?" begged Mr. Staplehurst. "I only want to ask you to be so kind as to say—before we go any further—who you are?"

The voice gave the reply with great distinctness.

"Jove?" repeated Staplehurst, "Jove what? Jove who?"

"Just Jove."

3

"What's your Christian name?" demanded Mr. Staplehurst aggrievedly.

"Haven't any thing to do with Christian names. I'm a god, and my name's Jove. You know me. Why, you wrote an article not long ago—a very good, sensible article—stating the facts of my case in a remarkably logical and admirable way. I—in fact I'm much obliged to you."

"That's all right," answered Mr. Staplehurst uneasily. "I'm glad you liked it; you needn't say any more about that."

"Oh, but I shall. It is not often I feel deeply over any thing, but your kindness"—the voice quavered a little—"your kindness really affected me very much. And now I understand that you have taken a brief on behalf of my wife, Juno. You have explained several matters in a way," the speaker coughed, "in a way that I must confess would never have occurred to me. I should say, Staplehurst, that you're a man who is making his way in the world."

"I began rather late," said Mr. Staplehurst. "I made mistakes when I was a youth, and in that way I lost time. If I had my time to live over again, I should know a great deal better what I ought to do."

"Still, you're all right now. Men should never worry about the past. It's the present and the future that count. And as regards the future, Juno, who is really very much touched by your kindness——"

"Where a lady is concerned," said Mr. Staplehurst lightly, "it behooves us all to see that her fair honor is not attacked by an ignorant rabble." ·

"That's just the way she put it herself. That's exactly what Juno said. But you are the first mortal who has troubled to take up the attitude, and Juno insists that we should do something for you."

"I couldn't really accept any thing. I'm very well paid for the——"

"Bosh !"

"I beg pardon ?"

"You don't know the kind of god with whom you have to deal. You have only to express a wish for something and, no matter what it is, I will see that it is done."

"Don't you trouble," begged Staplehurst. "I dare say there are plenty of people worse off than I am."

"That's not the question at all. We're talking about you, Gilbert Staplehurst, and we don't want a lot of other people brought into it.

Besides, if you lose this chance, you'll be sorry
for it. It will never come again. Now is your
time. Make haste."

" I don't want you to think I'm not grateful,"
said Staplehurst, with some anxiety, " but don't
you stop. I'm only wasting your time. Besides,
there's nothing that I really require just now."

"You're too modest by half. I can see that I
shall have to take this matter into my own hands.
You said that you wished you were young again.
You evidently want a chance of beginning life
once more, and of enjoying youth and happiness,
and——"

"That was only a wish," explained Mr. Staplehurst. "If it had been a possible thing, I might
not have thought of it."

" Don't talk of impossible things to me, sir.
It won't take me a moment. I'll do it, just to
show you that the gods can be grateful when they
like. Consider it done."

There was a noise as of the tubes being
replaced at the other end. A delightful sensation of virility went through Staplehurst's veins.
He let the tubes fall. The electric light went
suddenly out ; bright, fresh daylight came to
his eyes, and made him blink.

He stumbled, and recovered himself quickly. In a mirror at the opposite end of the room he had entered he saw his reflection; and a very pleasant reflection it seemed to be—a young face of a lad of twenty-two, plenty of dark hair, good complexion, in the eyes a quick, cheerful look.

" Hullo ! " he cried.

The carpet was nearly covered with slips of proofs, "pulls" of sketches, manuscript, and empty envelopes. In the corner was a waste-paper basket intended for the reception of these articles, but this held three siphons of soda-water. A large, square table stood in the middle, and this, too, was covered with literary matter, but with just a suspicion more of order in its disorder. A shaded lamp depended from the ceiling; the date-case in the corner was only about eight months behind; a huge Parisian advertisement, by Chéret, of a capering damsel was on one of the walls; and piles of blazingly new books stood like pyramids in three places.

The red, curly-headed man at the table looked up as Gilbert entered.

" Hullo, Gilbert! " said the man at the table, " you're late this morning, aren't you? Where have you been, old chap ? "

CHAPTER III

GILBERT stood for a moment on the doormat and gasped.

"I've had rather an upset," he said. "I can't explain it to you exactly, but——"

"That's a good thing," said the man at the table. "Start at once, will you, with this page, and go through it very carefully. As sure as my name is Bradley Webbe, we sha'n't get this thing tabled to-night. I am half inclined to chuck the whole business and run *amok* down the Strand."

Webbe took a cigarette from a tin box on the table, and lighted it at the end of the one which he was smoking.

"Aren't you enjoying life?" asked Gilbert.

"Are you?"

"I rather think," said Gilbert, glancing at himself in the mirror with increased satisfaction, "that I'm going to enjoy it very much indeed."

"Ah," said Webbe grudgingly, "you're young. You don't know what it is to be thirty-odd."

" Don't I ? "

" Thank your stars that you don't, Gilbert. Make the most of your time now. I've been in a lot of places in my time, but I never enjoyed myself anywhere so much as in the twenties." He looked up from the galley-proof which he was examining. " How do you spell *furieuse- ment*, Gilbert? The chap who writes this column uses the phrase every week, '*Ça donne furieusement à penser.*' I wish to goodness these fellows would stick to the English language."

Gilbert gave the information,

"Have you had your monthly check yet ?" demanded Webbe.

"Not yet."

" It will be in to-night, thank the Lord ! I want mine; you're different."

A sudden fear came over the new young man. He had little desire to start life again with no money at all in his pockets, and he went hastily through them to ascertain the extent of his re- sources. To his great relief, he found that the few sovereigns which were in his dress waistcoat before the change had been transferred to his present more free-and-easy tweed suit.

"Scott ! " cried Webbe.

"What's up?"

"You with five pounds in your pocket, and to-day pay-day!" The amazed Bradley Webbe affected to fall limp with astonishment. "My boy, you're becoming miserly."

"It's just as well to look after money, Webbe; you can't trust it to look after itself. Young fellows squander their cash a great deal too freely; if they would only save a little in their early youth, it would be so much better for them. There's an old Scotch adage——"

A "Whittaker's Almanac" caught the young lecturer on the arm and made him cease.

"I can stand a lot of things," said Webbe definitely, "but I can *not* and *will* not stand Scotch adages. Ring the bell, will you?"

A small, bare-headed, sombre-looking boy came in and took the slips which Webbe handed to him.

"Wait a moment, boy; Mr. Gilbert is nearly ready."

"Sha'n't be one minute," said Gilbert. "How's your mother, youngster?"

"Don't you begin chipping me, sir," said the small boy moodily. "I've got plenty to worry me without being chaffed. It's a licker to me how I get through it all."

"Cheer up, Barling," said Webbe encouragingly.

"It's all very well to *say* 'cheer up,'" said Master Barling, which increased gloom; "it's another fing to go and jolly well do it."

"I perceive," said Webbe, placing one leg over the arm of his chair, "that Miss Tomkins has been unkind."

"Onkind!" repeated the small Barling crossly—"onkind, you call it? If you awsk me, I should call it croolty to animals! 'Ere's me takin' that girl out Sunday after Sunday, givin' of 'er ices and chocolates and every thing the 'eart can wish for, and lawst Sunday what does she do but strolls out as cool as you like with [Master Barling gasped] 'Erry Rogers!"

"Barling," said Bradley Webbe with assumption of much interest, "surely you are not telling the truth."

"It's gawspel," said the boy, "gawspel. Goes out with 'Erry Rogers, that works round 'ere at Spottiswoode's; a chap—he ain't fifteen—a chap that can't smoke and don't know a race-'orse from a blooming 'air-pin." Master Barling rubbed his nose with the vague, wistful air of a man who cannot understand the orderings of

Providence. "But I know one thing and that ain't two. That girl——"

"Miss Tomkins?"

"That's 'er, sir. She can go down on 'er bended knees and beg and pray of me to keep company wif 'er again, but "—Master Barling frowned severely—"never no more. Once bit, twice shy. *She*'ll be sorry for it some day. The time 'll come when she——"

"Here you are, Barling," said Gilbert, handing over the corrected proofs.

"Thank you, sir." Master Barling came over and whispered confidentially to Gilbert. "Miss Reade is down stairs, sir."

"Really?"

"Talking to Mr. Besterton, sir. Thought I'd mention it."

"You did quite right," said the mystified Gilbert. And the small boy went.

"You might write a story on that," suggested Webbe, looking up from his writing. "That would rather suit your style, Gilbert."

"Oh," said Gilbert, "that's my style, is it?"

"It's a style," said Webbe candidly, "that, as you know, *I* can't get over."

"Too lofty?"

"Oh, dear, no! But still some people like it."

"I'm glad."

"And I dare say you'll improve as you get older."

"That's something to look forward to, isn't it?"

"Where you're lucky is in having the Proprietor on your side. And you've no relatives to borrow money from you, and—— In fact, Gilbert, you're a deucedly fortunate fellow altogether."

"Hooray!" remarked Gilbert calmly.

"Did that boy say that Kittie Reade was down stairs? She's really an exceedingly good sort. Clever, too, in her way. Her mother is tiresome, but some people are very unfortunate in the parents they choose. There's a subject for you. Do for a turnover for the *Globe*—'The Choice of Mothers.'"

"How old should you say Miss Reade was, Webbe?"

"You mean *is*."

"Yes."

"I should say that at her next birthday she would score twenty-two——"

"Twenty-three and not out," said a cheerful

young lady at the doorway. "If you *will* leave your door open, and if you *will* talk about ladies' ages, why——"

"I beg your pardon," said Bradley Webbe, rising from his chair hastily. "I didn't know you were there, Miss Reade."

"I can quite believe that." She turned to Gilbert. "And how are you?" she asked in a lower tone of voice.

"I haven't felt better for years," declared Gilbert joyously. "I am altogether like a new man."

"I'm glad you've changed," said Miss Reade quietly. "You said some unkind things last night at the Stewarts'."

"Did I? I didn't mean them."

Her pretty face brightened up at once. She placed the large envelope on the table, opened it, and took out the slips which it contained. She handed them to Bradley Webbe.

"What I like about 'Marianne's' columns is that they're always up to time," said Webbe. "It's never a case of 'It cometh not, she said,' with this 'Marianne.'"

"I am a most reliable young woman," said Miss Reade. "I always keep my promises.

This stuff signed 'Marianne' comes here on Wednesdays; on Fridays I have a column for a Sunday paper; on Mondays my column is ready for the other journal. And short stories thrown in!"

"You must earn very good money," said Gilbert.

"The money is good," she said quaintly, "but there is not always quite enough of it. Parents cost a good deal of money in one way and another."

She sighed a little.

"The pulls of your drawings will be here in a few minutes, Miss Reade," said Webbe, "if you don't mind waiting."

"Are you sure I shall not be in the way?"

"We like you to be in the way," remarked Gilbert.

She flushed and gave a comical little bow.

"How well some of these youths do pay compliments, don't they?" said Bradley Webbe admiringly. "I used to have a good manner with me when I was younger, but Gilbert beats me easily. I believe he studies 'Guides to Etiquette' and 'How the Upper Ten Behave,' and books like that! Am I right?"

"You are exhibiting all your usual accuracy," said Gilbert readily. He turned to the girl in the office chair. "Where are you going to-morrow evening, I wonder?"

"I shall be at home," she said. "If you were kind you would call and talk to mother for an hour. Or let her talk to you."

"I wish you'd write down the address," said Gilbert, "here on this slip. I always forget numbers."

"Thought you had a good head for figures," remarked Webbe, as Miss Reade took the pencil from her chatelaine and wrote. "You talked a good deal about Mrs. Brentford's."

Miss Reade looked up quickly.

"Do you know Mrs. Brentford?" she asked.

"Very slightly," declared Gilbert warily. "Is this the full address? No. 48 Alpha Terrace, Regent's Park."

The boy came, in reply to Webbe's ring, with the pulls of the costume pictures which were to accompany the ladies' page. Barling touched his forehead respectfully to Miss Reade, and that young lady looked with care at the impressions.

"That evening-dress sketch hasn't come out

very well," she said, "but it was not my best
work. This walking costume is right enough,
but I haven't got the trick of drawing for reduc-
tion yet."

"You always recognize your own faults,"
remarked Bradley Webbe, taking up his hat.

"Perhaps that's because there are so few of
them," remarked Gilbert.

"Isn't he simply perfect?" demanded Webbe.
"Doesn't he say lovely things, Miss Reade?"

"Sometimes," said Miss Reade. "Good-by,
Mr. Gilbert."

"Until to-morrow evening," said Gilbert, holding her hand for a moment. "I shall try to call
round at about eight."

"Do!" she said warmly. "Mr. Webbe, are
you going to see me into a 'bus?"

"That was the idea," said Webbe. "And I
want to make a call. I shall be back in half an
hour, Gilbert. You might write something, if
you will, that can be set up for next week in
case the advertisements don't come in thick.
Ready, Miss Reade?"

They went out and the door closed. Gilbert
resumed his seat and dipped his pen in the ink-
stand. He was thinking; thinking a good deal

of the young lady who had just left; he was wondering, too, whether he would find himself able to write with facility. He began to write the title.

"The Choice of——"

A swish of skirts behind him. Two hands on his eyes. The scent of a girl's hair. A whisper:

"Guess who?"

She snatched up the gloves which she had left on the table and hurried off. Gilbert, in a perfect glow of delight, went to adjust his dishevelled hair in the mirror.

"This is simply splendid!" he cried delightedly. "Why, I'm in love again!"

He had to walk up and down and around the office several times before composure returned. He experienced the joyful confusion of mind that comes to the youth whose heart is affected; a confusion which is too well known to everybody in this world to be here described at length. Moreover, to attempt to do so were only, perhaps, to expose the present writer's ignorance and to bring upon him contumely from the experienced.

Gilbert wrote as carefully as he could, and it

gratified him to observe that he retained the facility that he had enjoyed in his previous life. In reading over the fourteen hundred words which he managed to write before Bradley Webbe's return, one or two conceits in the thing almost made him laugh.

"What do you think of that, Webbe?" he demanded.

Webbe looked it through swiftly, reading apparently about six words on each page.

"Best thing you've done ; not half bad," he said, throwing it back. "I see that there's a Cabinet Minister resigned. We shall have to hunt up his portrait."

It was one of the great delights of the new life to find that, at lunch in the Strand, Gilbert no longer had to discriminate nervously between about three light dishes from the bill of fare, but that he could eat a good square meal with relish. An elderly man, sitting at the marble table opposite, looked at him enviously and sighed, and sipped at the lime juice at his side.

"Enjoyed your lunch, sir?" said the pretty waitress respectfully. She brought three cigars in a wine-glass, and brushed the crumbs from the table-cloth.

4

"I haven't enjoyed one to such an extent," declared Gilbert, "for twenty years."

The pretty waitress laughed so much that she had to put her hair straight.

"You young gentlemen do exaggerate," she said amusedly ; "one never knows whether you are speaking the truth or not. I don't believe you know yourselves half your time."

"Give me a light, Miss—Miss——"

"My name's Miss Bangs," she said, giving him the match, "B-a-n-g-s."

"It's a very charming name," said Gilbert pleasantly.

"It's a short name," confessed Miss Bangs; "it has that drawback."

"Oh, that doesn't matter. You won't use it long, I expect."

Miss Bangs looked around to see if any one else was demanding her attention. Every-body was apparently content, and Miss Bangs twisted her fringe and patted the white pinafore covering the bodice of her black dress, and smiled vaguely at an advertisement of a new kind of ginger-beer.

"Well," she said, "it doesn't become a girl to brag, but I must say I've had chances that many

another girl would have jumped at. There's
a gentleman now that mother's always urging
me to marry ; he's foreman in a warehouse—at
least, he isn't exactly foreman, but he's very near
to it—but," Miss Bangs sighed, "*I* don't know."
Miss Bangs glanced with something like admiration at the good-looking fellow to whom she was
speaking. "What *I* think you want is a loving
heart," said Miss Bangs.

"There's something in that," agreed Gilbert,
"but it is necessary to be circumspect. And
those of us who are young should lose no opportunity of endeavoring to find the one——"

"All right, sir," said Miss Bangs, to an impa-
tient customer. "I'll bring you some household bread in half a minute."

Gilbert discovered his own address in a book
at the *Budget* office, and when Bradley Webbe
told him he might go, he went outside a 'bus
from St. Martin's Lane to Bloomsbury in order
to see what the place was like. He found that
Doughty Street was a good broad street and
quiet, not far from the Foundling, and his
number looked even neater than the rest of the
houses. The landlady, sitting at the window of
the ground-floor room, bowed genially to him

over the wire blind, and he opened the door with the latch-key that he found in his pocket. In the hall was a bust of William Pitt with some one's straw hat set atop; a terra-cotta bust of Clytie, and a well-filled hat-stand.

"I was just goidg up to your roob, sir," said the small, neat servant with a cold in her head. "I was takig up this bustard to put id the cruet."

"Go on, Ermyntrude," said Gilbert.

"Jade, sir."

"I prefer to call you Ermyntrude for short."

It was really a very pleasant room. Two windows looking out on the street, a bedroom communicating, plenty of books about, a few ferns, an open piano.

"Bistress's cobplibedts, sir," said the small servant, "and will you dide id to-dight or dot?"

"I rather think I *will* dine in, to-night," said Gilbert, "if you can let me have something soon. I want to go out again."

"Goidg to a busic-hall, sir?" asked the small girl as she laid the cloth.

"I might, perhaps."

It seemed a sparkish, youthful thing to do; consonant with the acts of juvenility.

"I wedt last week, sir," said the small servant, placing a scrviette on the table, "and *I* dever saw adythidg so abusidg id all the days of by life. They *did* carry od. I believe it does ady body good to have a bit of ad outidg dow add agaid. What I bead to say is, it wakes you up, dod't it? Have you dode with your evedig paper, sir? I'll take it dowd to bistress. She likes to have a look through, just to read the burders."

Gilbert, dining from an excellent joint of beef, with a bottle of Beaune at his side, caught sight of himself in the large, shining sideboard at the end of the room, and stopping for a while, leaned back in his chair and laughed out of sheer joyousness.

"This is delightful!" he cried.

He busied himself after dinner in opening the drawers of the sideboard and gaining some idea of the extent of his possessions. For the small drawer in the writing-desk he could not find a key, and he had to leave that unopened. When he had finished his tour he sat down in the deep, easy chair, took from the convenient rack a pipe, and with some hesitation began to smoke.

"I've only had mild cigarettes lately," he said,

"I don't quite know whether I ought to venture on——"

But the pipe, like every thing else, was excellent to the taste of the young man. It soothed him, too, and as he sat there he looked hard at a portrait of a scarlet-faced general on the wall and thought.

"I'm going to make this a successful game," said Gilbert, between the puffs, "and of course I am going to enjoy life as well. With my experience I shall be able to avoid a good many of the blunders that are made by ordinary young men. I don't see," he placed one foot hard against the side of the mantle-piece, "I really don't see why I shouldn't do uncommonly well."

"Fidished your didder, sir?" asked the small maid, reappearing at the door.

"Yes, thank you, Ermyntrude. Oh, and I say, what time do the music-halls open?"

"About half-past seved," said Jane. "*We* got id early, by fred id the Arby ad be, because we wadted to have our bodeys worth. But a gedtlebad like you would just stroll id about half-past eight. By word, you do see sobe swells there, too. You *are* goidg, sir?"

"I feel that nothing in this world, Ermyntrude,

is just now of any importance except a music-hall. My heart's desire is to go to a music-hall. Until I have been to a music-hall, life has for me absolutely no attractions."

"I see what you bead, sir," said the small maid, taking the tray.

"I can get in at the front door all right at midnight, can't I?"

"Bid-dight or bid-day," said Ermyntrude, with some acerbity, "is all the sabe at this blessed place."

The music-hall was a revelation to Gilbert. He remembered that the last time he went to one, he had been bored almost to tears by the persistent idiocy of the performance. He saw at once that there had been a considerable im-provement, but there was, he knew, an improve-ment also in himself, and the good temper of every one affected his young head sympathetic-ally. When the song-and-dance lady came on, Gilbert found himself applauding, as vehemently as the rest of the folk in the circle, the not too abstruse song and the not too demure dance which she gave.

"This is the chap what'll give you fits," said a youth with a huge meerschaum cigar-holder, in

the next seat. The number was being changed
to a large "9" by a magnificent footman.
Through the slight haze of smoke Gilbert noticed
the boy distributing fresh books of music to the
hard-working orchestra. "He's a fair knock-
out, this chap is. I saw him once 'aving a drink
just like you or me might at a bar, and to look at
him you'd never guess he raked in fifty of the
best every week!"

"Fifty pounds?"

"Fifty solid pounds," said the informative
youth with the meerschaum cigar-holder.
"Fifty solid blooming sovereigns every blooming week of his blooming life."

The bell rang, the orchestra played a sym-
phony. It began to play it again, and as it did
so, a man came on in a confused uniform, with a
red nose, blue hair; a sword between his legs.

> "'Oh, I am a volunteer officer bold,
>   I'm always the first on parade;
> If sometimes I catch just a bit of a cold,
>   I don't care; I'm never afraid.'"

A small white cat strolled on the stage and
the comedian affected extreme fear. "Take it
away, man. You there with the calves. Drag

this 'orrible——" The magnificent footman
came on and took away the small white cat.
The hall roared at the carefully prepared joke,
and the red-nosed man marched to the chorus,

" ' When the enemy comes over, you will find me down at
    Dover ;
I shall only have to look at them and they will surely flee.
I shall argue with them kindly; then run away quite blindly.
If there's any body wounded, why——' "

(with much determination)

" ' it won't be me ! ' "

Then a long string of preposterous patter, at
which Gilbert found himself laughing as loudly
as any one.

He enjoyed, too, the musical clowns who
played on every thing excepting musical instru-
ments, and the precocious infant in evening dress
who sang,

" ' We are the boys that make a noise,
    At three o'clock in the morning.' "

The large, *décolletée* lady who sang songs of un-
certain sentiment about leaving her own sailor
boy, who'd gone across the sea ; the bicyclist,
who, at the end of his ten minutes' turn during

which he had bit by bit discarded his bicycle,
rode round on half of one wheel of his machine
without the spokes; the girls with raucous voices
and amazing vitality who shouted till they
themselves were hoarse, and kicked till every
one else was tired. Gilbert liked them all.

The gas was out in his room in Doughty Street
when he returned. He felt in his waistcoat
pocket for a light, and found there, in addition
to a small silver match-box, a key. It looked
like the key of the small drawer in the writing-
desk, and he went at once to try it before lighting the gas.

The lid opened, and a long, narrow, white-
covered book lay on the top. It was a bank
pass-book, and Gilbert struck a wax vesta and
turned over the leaves.

"Balance to credit account, £1852."

"Well," said Gilbert, with great complacency,
"no one can say that I haven't a fair start."

CHAPTER IV

At Lord's the following day, where Gilbert went to write for the *Budget* a descriptive sketch of the game, he, by the merest accident, met a man who apparently knew all about matters financial. He was a big, bald man, in a frock-coat that bulged unevenly, and he asked Gilbert, as they were standing under the clock, for a match. He lighted a long, expensive-looking cigar, and puffed up at the blue sky as though he were furnishing the blue sky with a new cloud.

"What I like about a cricket field," said the frock-coated man expansively, "is that everybody's hail-fellow-well-met. Now, that's me all the world over. I like to look upon every one of my fellow-men as a friend, but hang it, sir, how am I met? Eh? How am I met?"

Gilbert, with the modesty of youth, hesitated to offer a solution.

"Why," said the frock-coated man fiercely, "by suspicion, by doubt, by hesitation, by want of confidence, by, in short, a general exhibition of those confounded traits that are sending old England to the dogs."

He looked out at the play. "Well fielded, sir, well fielded!" he shouted approvingly. He turned again to Gilbert.

"Sending the good old country to the dogs, sir," he repeated.

"You think that is so?" enquired Gilbert respectfully.

"Good gad, sir," cried the other explosively; "I don't think. I never do think—I *know!*"

"That, of course," said Gilbert apologetically, "makes all the difference."

"Perhaps you're not an army man yourself," suggested the frock-coated man.

"I labor under the disadvantage of *not* being an army man."

"Ah!" said the frock-coated man, "as I expected. *As* I expected. There's a lack of decision about civilians that always betrays them. Now I'm a man who always hits the nail right on the head."

"Very good place to hit it," said Gilbert.

"Right on the head, sir," he repeated insistently. "I remember in the old days at mess, if there was any dispute on any subject the boys always said, 'Where's Dann? Go and find Dann, somebody. He'll settle it.' And by gad, sir, what Captain Dann couldn't settle, wasn't worth settling."

"There's room in the world," said Gilbert politely, "for men with heads."

"I'm in the City now," said Captain Dann, sending another cloud up to the sky, "and a pretty set they are there?"

"You don't mean in a physical way?"

"When I say a pretty set," said Captain Dann, behind his hand confidentially, "I mean a pretty bad set. Some of them will get stopped at it some day, you mark my words. Things can't go on for ever as they are going on now. There must be a stop sooner or later. Do you take any interest in business matters, sir?"

"I shall have to take a little."

"There are several things being floated in the City now that will never swim. They'll never swim, sir. They'll sink as soon as they are launched."

"Hard on the subscribers."

"I've no pity for them," declared Captain Dann obstinately. "No pity for them at all. If they'd only come and ask some of us we could warn them where they should not invest, and we could do more than that."

"Tell them where they should invest?"

"By gad, sir, you've hit it at once. You've got an old head on young shoulders, I can see. Tell them where they should invest. That precisely describes it."

"I want to invest a little money in something safe at about five per cent. It's in the bank at present, and I see they only give me two."

"All banks, sir," said Captain Dann, "are swindles."

"And if there's any thing going shortly that is really safe, and promises a fair dividend, I shall transfer some of it."

The man at the Nursery end cut a ball to leg. It was a boundary hit, and the lookers-on applauded in the modest manner that is usual at Lord's. Captain Dann offered his cigar-case.

"Some of the best, sir," he said. "Take one and try it. I like to meet with young men of sense. I always argue that they ought to be encouraged. Hope we shall meet again."

"I hope so, too."

"Here's my card. That's my address in the corner. If ever you want a bit of advice from a man of the world who knows the ropes, drop me a line and make an appointment."

" You're very good, Captain Dann."

" It's my nature," said Captain Dann excusingly. " We are what we are in this world, and there's no getting away from that. You can't fight against the eternal laws of Nature, sir."

Gilbert did not quite understand what this meant, but he said he supposed that was so.

"Nature," said Captain Dann, speaking as though Nature were a *protégé* of his, whom he was anxious to push into prominence—"Nature, sir, won't be trifled with. You can't do what you like with Nature. Nature is one of those things that gets its own way, and you may kick, and you may squeal, and you may scream, but—— Is this your card ? Thanks."

Captain Dann fixed his *pince-nez* and read it with wrinkled forehead.

" ' Doughty Street, Bloomsbury,' " he said.

" A mere journalist," explained Gilbert, " cannot afford to live in Carlton House Terrace."

" A journalist, sir," exclaimed Captain Dann, mopping his forehead and looking fiercely at the clock—"a journalist follows the best and the noblest profession in the world, and he can live where he deuced well pleases. He wields the pen that carries the news of England's greatness to—er—all ends of the world. All ends of the world, sir. In fact," here he took Gilbert confidentially aside and whispered, "in fact, as I once put it, speaking after a dinner where some press fellows were, the pen is quite as mighty, in of course a different way, as the—er—sword."

He shook hands with much pleasantness and told Gilbert that he believed Gilbert was going to make his mark in the world. He said "good-day" several times over, and went away toward the exit gate into St. John's Wood Road humming a cheerful tune, and leaving Gilbert with a vague feeling of gratification.

Gilbert strolled along to the press-box, and from a good-natured youth there obtained one or two facts. He noted also a few incidents on the ground; listened to the talk of a few *habitués*, and then felt secure in having obtained all the solid matter that was necessary. Too many facts always hamper a descriptive writer.

"I wonder whether there is any body here whom I know?" he said to himself.

It was the one circumstance in this new life of his which was disconcerting. The only plan was to nod to folk who nodded to him, and to reciprocate any and every sign of amiability. When, therefore, he found himself, just as he was about to leave the ground, hailed by an insistent voice, he turned at once, and finding that the owner of the voice was a smartly dressed, attractive lady standing up in a landau, he raised his hat.

"Come here at once, Mr. Gilbert!" cried the attractive lady. "How dare you leave without saying 'How d'you do?' to me?"

"Mrs. Brentford is not in the habit of being overlooked," remarked languidly a stout youth, standing with one foot on the step.

"I am very pleased to say 'How d'you do?'" said Gilbert. "What is the answer to the question?"

"The answer is that I am very much annoyed," said Mrs. Brentford, with a comic affectation of wrath. "Why didn't you come to my last At Home, Mr. Gilbert? Why should women any longer be trampled upon by brutes in the guise of men? Is it of any use writing to the *Times*, I wonder, or shall I get a member to move the adjournment of the House?"

"I wouldn't take any hasty steps," said Gilbert. "The fact of the matter is, I have been

5

very busy lately over an—an unexpected stroke of luck."

"Come next Thursday, then," said Mrs. Brentford. " Bring Bradley Webbe."

"Shall I dress in sackcloth and ashes, Mrs. Brentford ? "

" It is not a fancy-dress affair. You know Mr. Lancing, the artist, I think ? "

Mr. Lancing, the stout youth, shook hands, high in the air, and sighed after the exertion as though it had nearly exhausted him.

" Oxford man ? " asked Mr. Lancing.

" Don't think so," said Gilbert.

" Ah! " said Mr. Lancing compassionately.

" Tell me exactly how the game is now, Mr. Gilbert; and then we will go. I can give you a lift as far as civilization."

Gilbert did as he was desired. She seemed a very agreeable person, and the fact that she spoke with restraint to the stout Lancing served to accentuate her amiability. She was, perhaps, nearly thirty (which is by some considered to be the only real crime that a woman can commit); but the new youth did not consider that a drawback. It gave her a genial elder-sister air that was not displeasing.

"Home," said Mrs. Brentford.

A quiet, confidential chat on the way down to Marble Arch, that by adroit management on the part of Gilbert gave him a deal of information, and helped to place him to some extent *au courant.*

"I consider," said Mrs. Brentford, touching his hand with her parasol, "that you have good prospects, Mr. Gilbert, if you are only careful."

"Oh, I shall be careful!"

"You do hear of young men doing such stupid things, though. There seems to come a moment in their lives when they throw all discretion, all common sense, to the winds."

"It's very silly of them, Mrs. Brentford."

"Usually," said Mrs. Brentford hesitatingly, "it's over some girl. Some chit of a girl, on whom the rest of the world looks quite calmly, suddenly appears on the scene, and turns the poor young man's head completely round."

She smoothed the lap of her dress, and glanced at a well-dressed woman driving by.

"Still," urged Gilbert respectfully, "there are men whose heads are screwed on the right way."

"I hope so."

"Hasn't experience told you that, Mrs. Brentford?"

"I can't say that it has. Poor Mr. Brentford was one of the *queerest* of men. He had the most eccentric ways of running abroad, and running to Scotland, and running to America; and I don't know where he didn't run. He was never happy at home."

"I can't understand that," said Gilbert.

Mrs. Brentford gave Gilbert one of her impressive looks, and then looked down shyly at her small shoes and sighed. She was certainly a striking woman, and the air of half-condescension, half-protection, with which she treated Gilbert somehow gratified the youth exceedingly.

"I shall be seeing some influential people this evening—people who have to do with the "— Mrs. Brentford whispered the name of a great journal; "and, if you care for it, I should like to speak of you and your work."

"That's exceedingly kind of you," said Gilbert enthusiastically. "I want to get on in the world, and I've made up my mind not to lose any chance of doing so. That's the only way, *I* think. It is by missing opportunities for hitting that you find, when you are bowled out, your score is not worth mentioning."

"You're *quite* right—quite right. And be sure to remember one thing."

"That is?"

"That you have a good friend in *me*. I'll do all I can to help you."

"I can't thank you enough," said Gilbert honestly. "I don't know why you should take so much interest in me; but that only makes me the more grateful. If I can ever show you how sincerely——"

"You see," she said hastily, "women are so much more business-like nowadays than they were. At one time they were a *quantité negligeable* in the serious business of life; but that is changed."

"I'm glad."

"Men no longer make faces at women who interest themselves in affairs; unless, of course, the women are silly, and I—well, I'm not silly."

"The reverse."

"Shall we walk across Hyde Park," she asked, "and send the carriage home? I am in the mood for a talk with you."

Gilbert looked at his watch.

"I can listen to you for half an hour," he said. "I wish I could do so for half a century."

"You say things," said Mrs. Brentford, stopping the carriage, "that you don't mean."

"I mean a good many things that I dare not say," answered Gilbert.

"Hush!" said Mrs. Brentford.

It was too early for the gathering of entertainers just within Marble Arch; but one speaker—a dusty, demented, elderly lady—was there, and she was speaking, in a kind of subdued scream, to one nursemaid and two boys and three babies on the injustice from which she was suffering.

"Oh, my fellow-sufferers!" cried the old lady, untying the black strings of her bonnet, and addressing more particularly the three babies— "oh, my fellow-sufferers! it's time some of us made a stand—I say it's time some of us made a stand. It's time some of us made a stand, and put our foot down, and let those in 'igh places see once for all that we are not to be trampled on. I 'old in my 'and a few papers bearing on my case, and I should like to read you some extracts in order that you may see exactly 'ow I've been treated."

She placed the small bag with no handle on the gravel, and tipped her bonnet to the back of her head. She fixed one of the white, fat, staring babies with a serious eye, and the fat baby seemed to make an effort to enter into the spirit of the game.

"In the year '69," began the dusty old lady—"in the year '69 the bank in which my trustees 'ad invested my money—trustees whom I do not 'esitate to refer to 'ere, in the light of day, as sheep in wolves' clothing—I mean to say——"

Gilbert walked across Prince's Gate way, with Mrs. Brentford. They were as nearly as possible of equal height. Mrs. Brentford walked with the grace that comes to those who have not disdained exercise in the days of early youth; a rustle, a swish of silken flounces, formed an accompaniment to the musical chattering of her voice.

"It's hard, I suppose, to feel that one has a grievance against the world," she said. "It must keep one always at a red-hot point. I think every-body ought to be happy."

"That sounds like a good suggestion," said Gilbert.

"If people would only keep up their spirits——"

"Isn't that rather like the old story, Mrs.

Brentford? The full nigger always says to the empty nigger, ' Keep a good heart.' "

"I suppose one ought not to dictate behavior to others. I know that even when I had the letter from the Consul telling me of poor, dear, eccentric Mr. Brentford's death I——"

"He died abroad?"

Mrs. Brentford took out an absurd belaced little handkerchief.

"Yes," she said, "abroad. He was always more or less abroad. A dear, good fellow, but *so* odd. And, of course, it was a great shock to me, but I didn't let it disturb me too much."

"Quite right," said Gilbert approvingly.

"And although sometimes, of course, I feel lonely," Mrs. Brentford sighed, and put the little handkerchief back into its resting place, "still, I don't allow the feeling to affect me for long."

"You are well off?" guessed Gilbert.

"Oh, yes! Oh, dear, yes!"

"Even people who are well off are sometimes happy."

"Money," said Mrs. Brentford, "is not an absolute bar. How do you do?" Mrs. Brentford bowed with an indulgent air to some one who was hastening across the grass with a book under her arm to Hyde Park Corner. The hastening young person stopped, and the color came quickly to her pretty cheeks.

" I can't stop," she said. "How are you, Mr. Gilbert ? I have an appointment with an editor man, and you know what they are ! "

" We won't detain you, Miss Reade," said Mrs. Brentford politely. " Plenty of work ? "

" Miss Reade is always busy," said Gilbert.

" It is the better plan," said the young lady with spirit. "The idle folk get into mischief, and then busy people have to get them out of it."

" A poet named Watts," remarked Gilbert, " has put the same argument rather neatly. I haven't his poems with me, but I believe they include a reference to Satan. Are you going Strand way, Miss Reade ? "

" 'Bus from the corner," said the young lady promptly.

" Then if Mrs. Brentford doesn't mind I think I'll come with you. You can manage alone, can't you, Mrs. Brentford ? "

" Quite well," she said.

" And you won't forget to speak to that man about me ? "

" I will be sure not to forget. Good-by."

They were near to the band-stand. Mrs. Brentford shook hands, lifted her skirt slightly, and walked across Rotten Row. Gilbert and Miss Reade turned east. They walked along for some little time without speaking, and when, eventually, Gilbert remarked that he had been to Lord's to see cricket, his companion said, " Oh! " as though the statement interested her not at all. A long, tired man was asleep on one of the seats with his legs extended, and Miss Reade would have tripped over his feet, if Gilbert had not touched her arm.

" Please forgive me," she said quickly.

" For what ? "

"For being a silly, humpish young person. It only lasts two minutes with me."

" Two minutes is long enough."

" It is much too long," cried the young lady self-reproachingly. " It sha'n't happen again."

"Was there any cause for it ?" enquired Gilbert; "because, if so, we will remove it."

She stopped and laughed, and with a quick return to good temper, pointed to the tall figure of the far-off Mrs. Brentford. She assumed the frown, and stamped the stamp, of a tragic actress.

"Look, sir!" she exclaimed. Gilbert followed the direction. "That, *that* is the cause." She changed quickly to her ordinary self. "And now let's get on the top of a 'bus and forget all about her."

CHAPTER V

THERE were several matters in which Gilbert felt that his previous experience was of value. When, for instance, he received at his rooms a long letter from the effusive Captain Dann, begging him to come and see him at once on matters connected with an investment, he called down at the big block of buildings and went up the continuous lift, armed with a prudence that is generally associated with maturity.

Similarly, he thought as he waited in the outer office—Captain Dann always kept every-body waiting for five minutes, in order to convey an impression that he was engaged on matters of the first importance—in that five minutes Gilbert stroked his young mustache and smiled confidently at his reflection in a mirror, and decided that, in regard to any love affair that might develop, he would exercise identical foresight.

"I like little Reade," he said thoughtfully; "she's quite the dearest girl I have met. Pretty, too, and clever. And Mrs. Brentford seems amiable, and she lives at Queen's Gate and has no mother. The affair will require to be looked at squarely and calmly."

He whistled softly and half closed his eyes.

"The way is," he said argumentatively, to a map of South Africa that hung on the walls— "the way is to detach yourself from your own personal emotions and to do every thing according to the rules of a business-like man. The mistakes that I made before were due entirely to want of experi——"

"Captain Dann can see you now, sir."

The junior clerk gave the information confidentially, as something not to be bruited about.

"My dear fellow!" Captain Dann met Gilbert on the mat with an air of effusive delight, and held his hand for a few moments. "I'm awfully glad you called—for your sake. This is a moment that you will look back upon some day as the one which laid the foundation of your fortune. First of all, though, let me say this. You newspaper Johnnies—by the bye, this is my dear old friend Matcham. You must have heard of Matcham?"

That young man, with small eyes and no chin worth mentioning, nodded his head to Gilbert and said brusquely, in reply to Gilbert's enquiry, that he was feeling pretty fit. Rather thick night of it though, last night (said Mr. Matcham). Out with about ten chaps ; ten of the best. Painted (said Mr. Matcham with a mere flicker of satisfaction)—painted the bally place scarlet.

"My young friend Matcham," said Captain Dann excusingly, "is one of those who combine strictly business tactics with the—the *flaneur*, the *boulevardier*, the—to use a common expression—the man of the world. A many-sided man, Matcham,"—Captain Dann looked at the small-eyed youth critically,—"one who will some day make a mark."

"No necessity to make a mark," said Mr. Matcham, "when one can write one's name."

"Good !" cried Captain Dann explosively. "Devilish good. Mark—signature, good ! See it, Mr. Gilbert ?"

Gilbert answered that he had not failed to do so.

"Fine thing, humor, sir," said Captain Dann, still chuckling. "I often wonder where the deuce we should be without it. I crack a joke myself, when I see half a chance. Many a time, bless my soul, in my old days, I've sat at mess,

and I assure you "—Captain Dann laughed boisterously—"I assure you, sir, that I've kept the
whole table in a roar. The whole table, sir."

"Only the table?" asked Mr. Matcham
languidly.

"But this isn't what I wanted to see you about,
Mr.—Mr.——"

"Gilbert."

" Yes, yes, of course. A deuced good name,
too. Deuced good name. There's more in a
name than some people think. Give a man a
good name, and they'll never hang him. No, sir."

"Now, why in the world, Dann," said Matcham—"why in the world don't you cut your
cackle and get to business? You've got as much
jaw as an old woman."

"Briefly, my dear sir," said Dann, "the point
is this. There are some very cheap mining
shares—Merry, Merry England—in the market
just now, and my friend Matcham and myself
have secured a good many of them. At any
moment they may go up—at any moment! You
never know with these things."

"*I* don't," said Gilbert candidly.

"But some of us," went on Captain Dann
mysteriously—"some of us do. I can't give you

all the details just now—better not, I think, Matcham ?"

Mr. Matcham replied that not a word must be breathed to a soul on any account.

"But what I *can* tell you is that, if you like to invest an odd thousand, we can oblige you by letting you stand in, and if all's well you'll be glad you seized the opportunity. Now then, take a few minutes to think over it. You're a sensible young fellow—much like I was myself at your age—and I "—Captain Dann spoke impulsively—"well, I like you. There !"

Captain Dann mopped his bald forehead with his handkerchief.

"I wear my heart upon my sleeve, as I once rather neatly put it," said Captain Dann; "heart upon my sleeve. Eh, Matcham?"

Mr. Matcham said that if you asked him, Captain Dann was a fool to himself.

"I can't help it," said Captain Dann recklessly. "My plain, John Blunt way has lost me a mint of money in my time, but—well, friendship can't be bought. That's the way I put it. Let me be surrounded by friends, and I ask no more. Blood, is thicker than water. What do you say on that point, Matcham ?"

Mr. Matcham said cautiously that it depended.

"Depended be hanged!" said Captain Dann boisterously. "A friend I'd trust to the further-most ends of the earth; an enemy"—Captain Dann swept a sheet of letter-paper off the table with an expressive action—"an enemy I wouldn't trust with a penny 'bus ticket!"

"Can you give me an hour to think this over?" asked Gilbert. "I don't want to do any thing without due consideration."

"It's twelve-twenty now," said Matcham, looking at his watch. "Wire us here by one-twenty, and not a moment later."

"Not a moment later!" echoed Captain Dann. "At one-thirty another man is coming, who will go down on his knees for them! On his knees, sir! Call back or wire."

"I will," said Gilbert, rising; "and in any case, many thanks for the trouble you're taking."

"It's no trouble," said Captain Dann. "I don't make trouble of this sort of thing. Last week I should no more have given you the chance of this good thing than to—to the man in the moon. Do you know why? eh?"

"Well, you didn't know me."

"That's *just* it. That's precisely the answer

6

I wanted. I'm a judge of character, mind you, and it isn't often I make mistakes. I remember when I first met my dear old chum Matcham——"

"Drop it!" said that gentleman warningly.

"In fact, to put it shortly, I'm one of those who can take one look at a man and say directly, without thinking, 'He's sound' or 'He's not sound.' See what my meaning is?"

"I think I see," said Gilbert. "Is this my hat?"

"Have a drink of some sort?" suggested Matcham, rolling a cigarette. "Dann, why don't you keep a bottle or two of fizz about the place? Shall I send out for some, or——"

"I never drink before dinner," said Gilbert hastily.

"Why, that's like Dann." said Mr. Matcham, "only he has dinner at 10 A. M., before he comes to the City."

Captain Dann could not have laughed more loudly if he had made this joke himself. He walked to the lift with Gilbert, patting him on the back encouragingly.

"You'll like Matcham," he said with much joviality. "Sort of chap that grows on one, you know. More you see him, more you like him."

"Oh !" said Gilbert.

"And as keen, sir, as keen—well, as keen as I am. And that's keen enough for all ordinary purposes. Good-by. Wire us sharp, mind. Between ourselves " (this confidentially, for fear the empty lift should hear), "I don't want this other man to get them. He's what I call a bounder. Now," obstinately, "what I cannot and will not stand is a bounder. Good-by."

Mr. Gilbert, journalist, with a little competence in the bank, felt relieved when he found himself in the open air of Queen Victoria Street. He applauded his excellent wariness at not being caught by the net that had been spread in his sight, and at a restaurant in Cheapside he had a long lemon squash with a lump of ice bobbing a-top, and congratulated himself.

A large panel photograph in a shop window made him stop for five minutes, because the girl's eyes were rather like those possessed by Miss Reade. There were other photographs in the window; photographs of eminent beauties placed there to be purchased by emotional City youths, who would bear them home triumphantly on pay day to Islington, to enliven and make joyous the mantle-piece of bed- and sitting-room combined.

Also there were photographs of humorous comedians in their favorite diverting attitudes, with an excerpt from the dramatic literature with which they were associated, as "Ah, Tottie! *I* saw you first," and "This is the 'ottest place I've ever been in," and "I wonder what's become of my wife's Ma?" Further, there were, to balance matters and to compensate for these hilarious ones, portraits of demure bishops, and portly aldermen, and others; all looking very well-satisfied with the world and inclined to be just a little wrath with those who questioned the correctness of this attitude.

But Gilbert only looked at the girl whose eyes resembled those of Miss Reade.

"And they're to be had up this morning," said a man behind him; "and I hope they both go for trial."

"Bad case?" asked a straw-hatted youth of the man.

"It *is* a bad case and it *isn't* a bad case, if you understand me. It's a job that a lot of people have lost their money in, that's certain. Whether these chaps have done any thing that makes them liable to the law is, of course, another matter?"

"At the Mansion House to-day?"

"At the Mansion House," said the man.
"Case ought to be on now."

"How'd it be," asked the straw-hatted youth,
"to drop in and see the fun?"

"Not half a bad idea," replied the other. "I was always rather chummy with Wentmore."

"Won't look like bad form?"

"Bad form be hanged!" said the man. "For my part, I was never a stickler for etiquette."

Gilbert looked at the clock and decided to also spare an hour to hear some of this case of which the two were speaking. It would be a good object lesson, and one probably that would assist him in his scheme of caution.

He bought a financial paper in the street and noticed that the Merry, Merry England shares were down low.

"'Oh, wise young judge!'" he quoted. And composed and despatched a telegram to Captain Dann of Mansion House Buildings, declining the offer.

He strolled on and, ascending the steps where a small, excited crowd had assembled, went through a passage to the Justice Room. An Alderman in his gown was on the high-backed chair, behind him the sword of justice. The tall jailer in uniform opened the lid behind the dock, and much as though he were offering a fresh course at a rather long dinner said, "Number eight and nine, Sir Donald. Richard Wentmore and Joseph Marks."

The crowd at the side of the small, square room shuffled its feet and stepped on each others' toes the better to see. The two men, well dressed, stood in the dock, the tall foot-man-like jailer whistled down the speaking-tube to the cells below, and a youthful counsel in a frock-coat, with gardenia, rose and bowed to the judge.

"*I* appear for Mr. Wentmore, Sir Donald."

"And," said the Alderman humorously, with a strong Scotch accent—"and a fine appearance ye make, Mr. Fenton. He's done well to engage ye."

The young counsel bowed again; the small crowd at the side smiled and the Alderman laughed inwardly, in a manner so repressed that it made him quite scarlet in the face.

"Is your name Wentmore?" he asked one of the well-dressed men in the dock.

"It is, your worship."

"I think," said the Alderman, "if ye went

more to the kirk and not sae much to the City, ye'd get into less trooble."

Court much diverted. The prisoners, especially, quite delighted at the Alderman's humor.

"And your name," he addressed the other man, "your name is Marks."

"Joseph Marks, your worship."

The Alderman thought for a moment before offering his comment.

"It's only bad marks that coom to this coort," he said genially. "If ye were good marks, ye'd not have coom within a hoondred miles o' the place."

Court again amused.

"*I* appear for the Treasury, Sir Donald," said a bearded counsel briskly. "And I have to charge the two gentlemen in the dock with fraudulently obtaining money in the matter of a certain company, under false pretences. It is contended that there were incorrect statements in the prospectus issued by the prisoners——"

"False statement in a coompany proospectus?" said the Alderman, with comic affectation of amazement. "Where will this awfu' habit of leeing stop?"

"And I shall endeavor to give you evidence this morning that will enable you to commit the prisoners."

"I'll coommit the preesoners," said the watchful humorist in the high-backed chair—"I'll coommit the preesoners, if I find they've coommitted theirsel's a'ready."

Gilbert became interested in the case. It seemed an apposite illustration of the scene in which he had recently taken part, and the piling up of evidence against the two gave him intense gratification. The line of the younger counsel was that his client, Wentmore, was a man ignorant of these matters, who had allowed himself to be directed by the prisoner Marks.

"That's no excuse," whispered Gilbert to the man next him.

"Of course not."

"If a man is fool enough to assist a rogue to take in other fools, he must be punished for it."

"Quite so."

"I always contend, you know——"

"Silence there, please," said the Usher.

The excellent Alderman presently stopped the case. He had offered so many witticisms in the course of the hearing that the two men in the dock looked cheerfully and optimistically toward him.

"It's a verra interesting case," he said, "but I think I'll nae trouble ye to gie us any more of it."

The clerk stood up and whispered.

"Pairfectly so," said the Alderman. He turned genially to the prisoners. "I don't think we need boother much longer with this affair. I dare say ye're both extremely sorry that any body should ha' lost mooney o'er this beesness."

"Very sorry, your worship," they said in duet; "very sorry indeed. If we can do any thing——"

"Ye'll hae a guid opportunity of doing something later on, I'm thinking. I commit ye both for trial at the Old Bailey, and," he turned to the clerk, "I hope that they'll be severely punished for their behavior. Next case, please."

Gilbert, at the *Budget* office that evening, talked the affair over with Bradley Webbe and took much credit to himself for his acumen in avoiding the snares of Captain Dann and Mr. Matcham. Bradley Webbe remarked in answer that Gilbert's column wanted brightening up, and that even the Proprietor, with all his admiration for Gilbert's work, had confessed that it might be improved.

"An ordinary young man," went on Gilbert, "would have sat down and written at once a check for a thousand pounds, had the stuff transferred to him, and would have been the poorer by that thousand pounds and the richer for a few pounds of waste paper."

"I rather think," said Bradley Webbe, "that the Proprietor wants you to dine with him in Cavendish Square to have a talk with you."

"And what will happen when I dine with him, Webbe?"

"Why, you will begin at eight-thirty," explained Webbe, "soup and sherry. At nine you will find yourself at saddle of mutton and champagne. At ten liqueurs and cigars. At eleven, to the minute, out you go."

"Sounds all right."

"It *is* all right," said Webbe; "and if you can only play the amiable and keep on the right side of the old fellow, why you can't go far wrong."

"I don't mean to go wrong at all," said Gilbert confidently; "and you may be quite sure that I shall make myself agreeable."

"It's no effort for you to do so," remarked Webbe, "that's where you're lucky again."

"Again!" echoed Gilbert. "Have I been lucky in any other way?"

"All your life," said Webbe. "I think you are one of those men whose career is all mapped out and arranged, and all you have to do is to keep the rudder straight and go on. Where's that short story that came in this morning from young Lady Thing-me-bob?"

"I stuck it there to keep the window open."

"We mustn't lose sight of it," remarked Webbe. "It will have to go back by to-night's post. The young aristocracy, when they write, are like nothing else under the sun. They can't bear their precious scrip to be out of their sight for more than a few minutes at a time."

They wrote for a while without further conversation. Presently Bradley Webbe rang and Master Barling appeared. Master Barling rolled up the *Halfpenny Wonder* with a sigh, and placed it in the pocket of his corduroy trousers.

"Barling!"

"Sir, to you."

"Latest *Pall Mall*."

"Right, sir."

Bradley Webbe, when the journal arrived, leaned one leg over the arm of his office chair and went through the news rapidly.

"You see," said Gilbert, looking up from his work, "the best of being cool-headed is that you are prepared for the swindlers in this life."

"What are you talking about now?"

"Why, in regard to this Merry, Merry England mine. One would have thought, to hear Captain Dann talk, that really it was one of the most profitable investments that any body could put their money into. 'A fortune in it, my boy,' he said. But I was just a little too knowing for them, I fancy. I wasn't born yesterday, Webbe."

"Did you tell them so? These little facts are very impressive sometimes."

"I didn't tell them, but I expect they saw they had a wary customer to deal with. Why, the very name of the mine is against it. Merry, Merry England indeed! Merry, Merry swindle I should call it."

Webbe turned over to the City page.

"Hullo!" he exclaimed.

"I wonder where they find their victims, these chaps," went on Gilbert. "You'd think that at this end of the century, now—— What's the matter with you, Webbe?"

"Nothing the matter with me," said Bradley Webbe; "nothing the matter with the Merry, Merry England shares. On the contrary, listen to this."

Gilbert, amused, turned to listen.

"'A most gratifying cablegram reached Throgmorton Street this afternoon from the Merry, Merry England Mines. We are not able to give a literal copy, but the effect is that a new vein of gold has been unexpectedly struck, and this scheme, which has for some months past been down at the bottom of the list, will once again take up position. A tremendous bound upward in prices naturally took place, and lucky outside buyers of shares at the figure of the last few months will make a big haul. As it is, nearly every-body who "knew any thing" in financial circles had unloaded the shares long since.'"

Gilbert rose from his chair and went to the window. He opened it and stood there for a few moments. The voices of printers' boys came up from below and mingled with the tinkling of a piano-organ out in the street. Two or three murky-faced infants were pirouetting to the gavotte, stopping now and again to pull up their socks and to ask the beaming Italian gentleman why he didn't turn the handle faster.

"Come on," said Bradley Webbe ; "don't dwell on lost opportunities, there's nothing concrete about them. Do you happen to know whom Dom Pedro married ?"

CHAPTER VI

THE immediate acceptance of a five-thousand-
word story by one of the weeklies—he was free
to work for papers other than the *Budget*—sent
Gilbert into a state of delight that helped to compensate for the disappointment caused by the
Merry, Merry England affair. He had not experienced this acute satisfaction for so many
years that he had quite forgotten its joyousness.
Now he remembered that, in the old days, the
feeling of desolation which came when the servant handed in large, white envelopes was always
atoned for by the sensation of supreme content
that occasional letters of acceptance brought.

At these times the buoyant-minded recipient
feels so assured that his pathway to success is
broad and smoothly paved that he generally goes
and buys a new necktie. Gilbert's feeling was
that he must tell somebody of the incident at
once ; somebody who would be pleased to hear
it and who would frankly say so. And he took
'bus straightway to Portland Road Station and
called at Alpha Terrace.

"This *is* good of you," said Kittie Reade. She rose from the table at which she was working and came to take his hat and stick. "I was afraid you were annoyed at poor mamma's remark the other night and that we shouldn't see you again."

Gilbert laughed good-temperedly.

"Is Mrs. Reade in?"

"Mamma is playing at nap," said Kittie brightly. "She always has just forty winks at midday. Do you mind if I go on with my work? You can talk, you know. It won't affect me."

"Can nothing I say affect you?"

"I didn't mean that," she said composedly.

She resumed her seat at the small table and went on with her sketch of "A New Morning Frock." Gilbert told her of the acceptance of the short story, and she flushed prettily with delight.

"And I think it would show Providence that I am grateful," said Gilbert, "if I were to do something in a special way to celebrate the event. Where could we go now in order to spend a happy day?"

Kittie Reade tapped her lips with her pencil and rocked back in the chair and considered.

"Rosherville!" she cried suddenly.

"Very well," agreed Gilbert; "but isn't it rather——"

"I don't know," said Kittie; "I've never been there. We'll take mamma and——"

"Do you think she will enjoy it?"

"Oh, yes!" said Kittie hastily, "she will like it very much. And we'll go by the three o'clock boat from London Bridge, and have tea in the gardens and roam about and see every thing that's funny and come back, too, by boat." She hesitated a moment. "It won't be expensive," she added.

"That's a drawback," said Gilbert, "but for once we must put up with it. Give my regards to Mrs. Reade. At three o'clock sharp, mind, at London Bridge."

"I shall just be able to finish my sketch in time."

"Do you never neglect your work?"

"I am the most reliable young person in the world," said Kittie Reade quaintly. "Good-by until three."

At three o'clock, therefore, the Swan pier near London Bridge: London Bridge itself fringed with heads of leisurely loafers who lean elbows on the stone coping and conjure up a kind of abstract fatigue by watching the work of the men on the boats below; London Bridge also busy with 'bus and wagon traffic, anxious to show Tower Bridge that it still finds plenty to do, in spite of unmannerly competitors with bascules and other fal-de-lals.

The *Swiftsure* bumped gently at the side of the pier, and across the gangway to the *Swiftsure* walked intending voyagers, the four members of the band watching each narrowly, as who should consider *"Are* you good for a tanner, or are you *not* good for a tanner?" A fussy little steamer came across from the Southwark side of the river to take passengers to Chelsea, and became very excited and frothed furiously at the paddle-wheels on finding the *Swiftsure* slightly in the way.

"Plenty of time," cried Gilbert. "How do, Mrs. Reade? I've got the tickets. This way."

Kittie Reade, in absolutely the neatest and most charming of tailor-made gray serge gowns that mortal tailor ever cut, and a big-brimmed hat fixed with a silver stiletto, gave her arm to the elder lady.

"Don't for goodness' sake ask me how I do,"

Mrs. Reade panted. "Do *please* let me sit down first and get my breath. Young people nowadays seem to have *no* consideration, really. To please them you must be always flying here or flying there, trapsing *up* steps and *down* steps and——"

"You sit here, mamma," said Kittie gently, "and you'll be nicely sheltered from the wind."

"Nicely sheltered, indeed!" said the lady wrathfully. "There's a lot of 'nicely sheltered' about this business."

"The mood only lasts a few minutes," whispered Kittie apologetically to Gilbert.

"I know."

Gilbert turned to Mrs. Reade.

"Do you mind if I say a very rude thing, Mrs. Reade? I want to tell you that this new bonnet of yours simply makes you look ten years younger."

"Oh, Mr. Gilbert!" said the old lady delightedly, "how *can* you say such things? But really, do you think it suits me?"

"It has such a *chic* appearance!" urged Gilbert.

"*I* thought it seemed a little too young," she said doubtfully.

"My *dear* Mrs. Reade! In these things every thing depends on the wearer."

"Well," acknowledged Mrs. Reade candidly, "there certainly *is* something in that. I once had a sister who, just because she married a colonial man, seemed to think she was every-body, and that sister of mine, if you'll believe me, never *would* take my advice in matters of dress."

"Good gracious!" exclaimed the surprised Gilbert.

"The trouble I used to take over her, too! *I* never saw her equal, really. And this just shows that it's no use trying *too* much. There was *she*, an ordinary girl,—she had none of the good looks, bless you, of the rest of us,—and this sheep-shearer, or whatever he was, came over for a holiday from Queensland, and he had plenty of money, and I'm sure the poor silly man could have had the pick of us; instead of which——"

"Chose her!"

"Chose her," confirmed Mrs. Reade.

"Well, well!" said Gilbert amazedly, "that's the most extraordinary anecdote I ever heard."

"Oh, bless you!" said Mrs. Reade lightly, "that's nothing. Why, there was a cousin of mine once—her name was Maude, but she was a pleasant enough young girl for all that—and she——"

The clock on the insurance office showed at three, and faint jingling of the hour came from City churches. The *Swiftsure* was comfortably full, and under the canvas-covered half of the deck the breeze danced refreshingly. A bell rang, and the *Swiftsure* backed away from the pier and then returned and bumped it once more for fun. The captain on the bridge called down the brass speaking-tube, the *Swiftsure* went out into mid-stream, selected an archway, and, its funnel lowered, went through it ; the band started a selection of comic songs hewn into quadrille form ; the men unloading mammoth blocks of ice at the wharves cheered ; a facetious youth on board affected to shed blinding tears at the agony of leaving his native land and waved good-by to a fictitious parent.

"But don't you let me go and take up all of your time, Mr. Gilbert. It's very good of you to ask us to come, I'm sure, and it would be too bad for me to talk and talk and talk all the while. Is there an inquest, or any thing, in that paper you've got ? "

Gilbert found a good long absorbing inquest

for Mrs. Reade, and that lady composed herself for an enjoyable read. Kittie and Gilbert walked along the deck and watched the wharves, the old-fashioned inns squeezed tightly between them, and the huge steamers, mid-river, unloading their cargo.

"We have here," remarked Kittie, with an imitation of the showman manner—"we have here Wapping Old Stairs, referred to in the olden days, you will remember, ladies and gentlemen, in immortal poetry that can never die. Also we have here the Thames Police Station, so called on account of it being the—er—Station of the Thames Police."

"Cheers!" remarked Gilbert.

"In the old smuggling days Wapping was a prosperous place, and a good trade in wines, spirit, and cigars was carried on to the satisfaction of all but King George's revenue men. Stowe tells us——"

A curious, clean-shaven man in convex glasses was watching them with much interest. She stopped her imitation at once.

"Pardon me, Miss," said Gilbert, as they walked along, "but how did you come to learn all you know?"

"The gentleman in the gallery asks me how I came to learn all I know. My reply to the gentleman is that I came to know *what* I know by keeping on pegging away, reading all that I could, and not—well," she resumed her normal manner, "not being lazy!"

"And are you happy?"

"Oh, yes! Certainly. Nearly always happy."

"But not quite always?"

"Why, nobody is always happy, Mr. Gilbert. It would become quite intolerable to be always smiling. Besides, if we were never miserable, we should not know, when happiness came, how pleasant it was."

"I wonder now," said Gilbert, looking thoughtfully at the folk on deck—"I wonder now whether there is any body on board this steamer who is seriously below the average in contentment. I suppose, if you weighed each case squarely, you would find that Providence has been pretty fair to every body."

The wind, coming round the bend of the river down to Greenwich, lifted a youth's straw hat and sent it out to sea. A long, deep roar of laughter came from a knot of men and girls standing near. The tears rolled down their cheeks as they watched the cross, indignant youth ; the ladies had to lean against the sides and fan themselves exhaustedly with their pocket-handkerchiefs.

"Now that, for instance," said Miss Reade— "that just shows how difficult it is to gauge the emotions of any one but one's self. That incident doesn't amuse me at all."

"Yet it has added to the gayety of nations," remarked Gilbert.

She looked out at the shipping in the docks; the masts as thick as hop-poles in Kent at summer time.

"Let's give it up," she said cheerfully. "What we must each of us do is to live our own life."

"That's it," agreed Gilbert excitedly; "fight for yourself and make your way in the world——"

"Yes."

"And if somebody should impede the way, why, somebody must go out of it, neck *and* crop! That's the plan that I——"

A toddling child in a stupendous, white, Beefeater hat came staggering with infantile recklessness across the gangway, and Gilbert, in his enthusiasm, would have stepped against it, if

Kittie had not lifted the small person aside. She gave the fat cheeks a kiss with a nice, feminine action and guided the tiny promenader to her young mother.

"But you must not forget to have consideration for others," she said sedately to Gilbert.

At Rosherville the *Swiftsure* released its passengers, and they went up to the gates and wandered about the grounds. The grounds were dusty grounds, to some extent; and a school party, which marched about with banners, raised a perfect simoom wherever it went. Mrs. Reade was much moved at the cordiality of the welcome which she spelled out on the ornamental flower-beds, and cried a little, as though the warmth of the gardener's gentle art had touched her acutely. A tired, unwashed old bear in a pit reminded her of a diverting incident in the Zoölogical Gardens in her young days and effected another change of temperament.

"Ah!" said Mrs. Reade, "time goes on, I say, Mr. Gilbert; time goes on, doesn't it?"

"There seems to be no means of stopping it," agreed Gilbert.

"Sit down here, mamma dear," suggested

Kittie; "this is rather a pleasant seat. You will get tired if you walk too much."

"I may be past my first bloom of youth," said the old lady with sudden *hauteur;* "I don't deny it; it would be useless to do so. I'm no longer a giddy-pated miss of eighteen; I acknowledge that frankly. But if a daughter of mine is to dictate to me exactly when and where——"

"Come along, then, mamma." Kittie always preserved her good temper with her mother. "I'll run you to the tea-room, and Mr. Gilbert shall be referee."   .

" *There* she goes," complained Mrs. Reade to Gilbert; "*there* she goes to the opposite extreme now. I cannot understand people who change about so. Who's this supposed to be, I wonder ?"

They looked at all the whitewashed busts on their way to the tea-room. Also they found at the end of the gardens a round, boarded space with members of the band perched high up in the centre as though they were birds, and dozens of couples dancing strenuously to the blatant waltz.

"Have I ever danced with you?" asked Gilbert.

" Of course you haven't. You know that."

" I didn't know," said Gilbert candidly. " Are
you engaged for this waltz ? "

" After tea, perhaps," she whispered; " when
mamma is asleep."

Nothing could exceed the frivolity and light-
heartedness of the excellent Mrs. Reade at the
tea-table. The jokes that versatile lady told;
the humorous comments that she made on the
appearance of a hard-faced, flat young waitress
who attended on them ! Mrs. Reade, searching
through the caves of memory, brought to light
astounding anecdotes of much length and some
obscureness, not entirely unconnected with one
Mr. X.; a gentleman to whom she begged permission to refer thus guardedly. It delighted
Gilbert to watch the admirable tact of Kittie
under these trying circumstances.

" And the Opera House at the time I'm speaking of," went on Mrs. Reade, pouring out her
fourth cup of tea, " was at *this* end of the Hay-
market, if you understand me, Mr. Gilbert ? "

" Perfectly, Mrs. Reade."

" And Mr. X. made a proposition to my
father, who was, although I say it, one of the
most punctilious men that you ever dreamed of.

Etiquette? My *dear* sir! You've heard of the Comte d'Orsay, perhaps?"

Gilbert nodded assent.

"Well," said the old lady impressively, "the Comte d'Orsay was, if you'll believe me, a mere bull in a china-shop compared with my poor father. A mere bull in a china-shop, I do assure you."

Gilbert said he could quite believe it.

"It was the talk of *all* Hornsey," declared Mrs. Reade with triumph. "To see him bow to Sir Henry, who lived up in the large house near the church—it used to astonish Sir Henry himself. Well, as I was saying—bless my soul, what *was* I saying? I get so interrupted when I do happen to open my mouth for a single moment that it's no wonder——"

"You were talking of Mr. X. and the Opera House, mamma."

"Of course I was! of course I was! Very well, then. This Mr. X., he called on poor papa and said would he allow Miss Mercy—that was me—to go to hear 'Puritani' with him. And so papa hummed and ha'd a bit, as any gentleman would, but at last he gave in."

"And you went to hear 'Puritani'?"

"*Do* wait a bit, *please*, Mr. Gilbert. If I don't tell the story my own way I shall never get through with it. Well, when the evening came, poor papa had been having a glass or two of port, as, of course, every gentleman who *was* a gentleman used to in those days, and when Mr. Brown called——"

The old lady stopped with sudden consternation.

"There !" she exclaimed; "that's *your* fault, Kittie."

"What, mamma ?"

"Why, making me blurt out the name of the gentleman that poor papa had a row with over me. Really, you *do* aggravate one !"

When Mrs. Reade consented after tea to doze, Gilbert and Kittie stole their dance on the boarded platform outside. The band aloft played a waltz, and the enchanted youth took the delighted young lady and footed it with the best of them. The rest of the dancers were partly Kentish damsels and their swains; partly their fellow-voyagers by the boat. A few of these stopped and stared open-mouthed at the well-dressed young couple waltzing in such inappropriate surroundings with so much enjoyment.

And Gilbert felt that now, indeed, he was experiencing the delights of youth.

"An odd sight, sir?"

Kittie had gone in to prepare her mother for the return journey. The convex-spectacled man leaned against a square post and stroked his clean-shaven chin. He spoke with a queer, nervous air.

"Yes," said Gilbert, fanning himself with his hat. "A little like the Continent, isn't it? The chalk walls over there make a good background for the trees."

"It wouldn't make a bad article for one of the evening papers."

"I'll do it!" cried Gilbert.

"You are a journalist? I used to do a little myself when I was young, but I came into some money and——"

"That was lucky."

"You're wrong, sir," declared the spectacled man. "Quite wrong. It was the very worst thing that could have happened. It is only by exercise of the greatest ingenuity that I can prevent myself from being a miserable man."

"But you do manage to evade it?"

The band started in its lofty perch a polka.

There were some at the gardens who were coy
in regard to a waltz, and shirked the lancers
altogether, but it seemed that they could all
dance a polka. So crowded was the boarded floor
that couples bumped up against each other, and
went on good-humoredly, only to bump again.
The shrill giggling from the ladies was continuous.

"I am not quite sure," said the spectacled man.

The *Swiftsure* was obediently waiting at the
little pier when they came out of the gardens.
The convex-spectacled man, with a purse in his
hand, touched Kittie politely on the shoulder
and asked if her name was Katherine Reade.

"It is," said Gilbert with an air of proprietor-
ship.

"I found this small purse at the gate, with
this card in it," said the convex-spectacled man,
"and I thought I heard you call the elder lady
Mrs. Reade. And putting two and two together——"

"That is *so* good of you," said Kittie thank-
fully. "I should have been sorry to have lost
it entirely."

"I am glad to have been of some service,"
said the spectacled man. "I am not of very
much use in the world."

"I think that's almost a wicked thing to say," interposed Mrs. Reade graciously. "We all have our work to perform, even the meanest."

"Mamma, dear!"

The man lifted his hat to the ladies, and Gilbert shook hands with him and exchanged cards. The name on his card was Ford. They saw no more of him on the journey back.

A delightful voyage home. Noisy at first, with choruses at one end of the ship and gentlemen alternately quarrelling and swearing never-ending friendship; but these become quiescent after a while. A young moon, scarcely half formed, comes up and beams on the river; the stars in the dark blue sky are out in their fullest strength. Gilbert, sitting next to Kittie, finds that when, by accident, his foot touches for one moment her small, brown shoe, a swift rush of excitement makes him flush. He interrupts the remark he is making and looks at the eyes under the wide brim of her straw hat.

"Let me see," says Gilbert reflectively; "have I ever asked you to marry me, Kittie?"

The flower at her bodice stops for a moment its regular movement.

"There *was* some vague talk in regard to the

affair," she says, laughing a little nervously, "but I fancy nothing definite was settled."

"I didn't give you a ring?"

"Oh, dear, no! No."

" That was very thoughtless of me. I must remedy it as soon as possible. And, Kittie——"

"Yes."

"Shall we talk quite seriously for just one minute?"

"It's a long time," she says.

"Supposing I were to tell you that I care for you more than every other woman in the world? Supposing I were to tell you that with your help I should feel the more confident of making my way in the world. Supposing I were to tell you that I want to marry you soon—soon. Supposing I were to say that I believe you to be the dearest and the sweetest——"

"No, no," she whispers. "I'm only just a girl. Don't think I am any thing more."

"And will you marry me, dear love," he says anxiously, "as soon as I like?"

She looks across the deck at the winking eyes of the warehouses. A boat with the peak-capped, reefer-jacketed Thames Police comes alongside one of the huge Norwegian steamers,

8

and the sergeant, sitting at the bow, flashes the light of the lantern on the ship's side. The singing at the other end of the *Swiftsure* comes faintly now, for the singers are tired.

"Dear heart," she says softly, "I love you too well to say no!"

His lips have been very near, under the brim of her straw hat, to her little white ear. They are nearer now—and nearer.

"I believe, Gilbert," declares Kittie, putting her big hat straight, "that, with ordinary luck, we shall be a very happy young couple."

CHAPTER VII

THE feelings of an affianced youth on the morning following his engagement are said to be usually those of extreme satisfaction with the world. Proposals, it is notorious, are generally made at eventide; twilight has often been especially recommended by careful watchers of the game. The indecision of the atmosphere assists somehow to attune the mind to the desirable key. It is doubtless a want of knowledge of this that has sent so many men through life in the deplorable state of bachelorhood. They have asked for hearts and hands on foggy days; they have, perhaps, called quite early in the afternoon; they have chosen moments when all that the lady really required was, not a husband, but a cup of tea.

Gilbert, parting his hair with some accuracy before his mirror, looked thoughtfully at himself and flushed with pleasure as he thought of the previous evening. He picked out a necktie Kittie had once referred to appreciatively.

"Hullo!"

"It's odly Bister Webbe, sir," said Emyrntrude. "Shall I ask hib to wait?"

"Tell him to come in here," said Gilbert. And Bradley Webbe stamped into the bedroom.

"I say," said Webbe, "I want to go away for a week rather urgently, and I want you, Gilbert, to look out. You can manage, can't you? Lucas will give you a hand."

"I've got two already," said Gilbert. "When do you come back?"

"I sha'n't be longer than I can help, old chap. Fact is, there's some money affair going on down where my people used to live; and if it comes out right, it will be rather a fine thing for me."

"Good luck!" said Gilbert.

Gilbert waltzed a few steps to the cupboard for his coat:

"Anything happened?" asked Bradley Webbe.

"What do you mean?"

"This gayety of manner—this Gaiety Theatre manner—is not usual with you. You are generally a sedate youth."

Gilbert took Bradley Webbe's arm and led him into the sitting-room.

"Have *one* cup of coffee," he said; "and if you'll promise to keep the information secret, perhaps I'll tell you."

"Is it worth printing?" asked the journalist cautiously.

"Oh, no! It interests no one but the parties concerned."

"I've had breakfast," said Bradley Webbe, "and I want to be off; but your air of mystery, young sir, attracts me." He sat down with a fine mock melodramatic air. "Tell me the story, fair youth."

"Sugar?"

"Tons!" said Bradley Webbe.

They talked about the current number of the *Budget* and the relative value of the younger black-and-white artists. Bradley Webbe, being one of the shrewd fellows of this world, had ever a wary eye for youths who had not yet arrived.

"It won't be a bad number," said Webbe, summing up; "and so long as the Proprietor is satisfied, nothing matters."

"What would happen if he were not satisfied? I suppose he would stop the whole concern?"

"Capital, my dear Gilbert, is able to do just what it darn well likes."

"I shouldn't care to be thrown out of a berth just now," said Gilbert apprehensively. "That would lack all elements of fun."

"I, too, should feel more independent if I had money to fall back upon. You see"—Bradley Webbe turned and looked out of one of the windows—"one might get married."

"More than one. Say two."

"Well, two then. I suppose that is the correct total."

"But why get married? Has some one given you a white waistcoat?"

"The question has not yet arrived at that stage. In fact, I—I haven't asked the lady."

"You mustn't forget to do that," advised Gilbert. He took a second egg and tapped it to the rhythm of his quotation:

> "'Fair ladies by faint hearts were never won;
> Win their love swiftly, lest they turn and run.'"

"These matters are not to be settled," said Bradley Webbe, "by irresponsible youths of no experience."

"My good chap," said Gilbert joyously, "I

have had more experience in this world than——
I beg pardon. I ought not to brag. Does the
damsel like you ? "

" That's rather difficult to say—for certain."

" She has never thrown any thing at you ? "

Webbe shook his head.

" Come, now, that's encouraging. Can I help
the matter to a happy solution ? "

" Why, do you know, Gilbert," cried Webbe,
starting up, " I rather think you could. I can
rely on you ? "

" The Bank of England is, as compared to me,
a mere reed."

" You might help me," went on Webbe, speaking quickly, "by saying something to her about
me in a casual way when opportunity offered.
Of course, you wouldn't let her see that it was
intentional."

" Of course not."

" But a word or two might make a lot of difference. I'm not a bad sort of fellow, and I
think I should make a fairly good husband.
And I'm energetic and——"

" One moment, Webbe. I must put these
things down or I shall forget them."

" It sounds rather stupid, I know," said Webbe

apologetically, "but I'm rather anxious about the matter. It makes a lot of difference to a man whether he gets the wife he wants, or whether he gets one——"

"Whom nobody wants. Is there any thing else?"

"Let me think," said Bradley Webbe, with a pleasant laugh. "I had one or two other virtues, I think."

"Try your waistcoat pocket."

"Well, you might bear in mind generally that I'm steady, and" (Bradley Webbe ran his hand through his thick red hair, and laughed a little awkwardly) "and—I'm fairly honest, and——"

"You're a very good chap," said Gilbert earnestly, "and I'll do all I can. Are you off now? I sha'n't see you before you leave, I suppose?"

"I am going at once. Here's an address that you can send letters to. And don't forget to do that article on the Chinese shop, will you? We've got the illustrations."

"I—I was going to make a call, but I'll do it this evening—the Chinese thing. Good-by."

Bradley Webbe found his hat, and stood at the doorway.

"And, Gilbert; if you have a chance, you will do what I asked you?"

"There's only one detail that you have forgotten; you haven't mentioned the name."

"Haven't I really? Perhaps I thought you had guessed. But I quite thought I had mentioned that Miss Reade——"

"Kittie Reade?"

"I shall call her Kittie some day, if all goes well. Good-by, Gilbert. Keep a good look-out, won't you?"

The door closed, but the footsteps returned hurriedly.

"I say, Gilbert! I beg your pardon really. I'm absolutely selfish when I am thinking of this particular subject. What was your secret?"

"My secret!"

"You said you had something to tell me when I came in."

Gilbert went toward the excellent Webbe with much gravity of demeanor, and put his hand upon his shoulder.

"Since I spoke," said Gilbert, "the affairs of Europe have assumed a more complicated attitude, and it would ill become a wary Cabinet Minister like myself to disclose Imperial secrets.

The honorable member will therefore kindly allow me to postpone my answer to the question on the paper."

The door closed again on Webbe's good-tempered laugh. Gilbert whistled very slowly a rollicking air and took his pipe and his newspaper.

"Poor old Webbe!" he said with genuine concern. "Upon my word I feel quite sorry for him. But I'm glad the dearest possible is mine. I am not going to lose her."

Nevertheless it did occur to Gilbert, late in the day, that he had acted in a perfectly conventional manner in his affair of the heart; that he had exhibited none of the calmness and forethought which a man of his ripe experience should have exhibited. A note from Kittie, enclosing a cabinet photograph of herself, dispelled the shadow of these thoughts. It was such a very charming note that it was capable of doing almost any thing. Gilbert took an opportunity, when Master Barling left the room, to press the photograph to his lips and to place it with much care in his breast pocket. The arrival of the letter had, indeed, a most disturbing effect upon the infatuated youth. He found himself drawing

her face on the blotting-pad; he began a letter
to an archdeacon, returning a humorous story,
with "My dearest and loveliest girl," and
detected the clerical error just in time.

"If it wasn't for this confounded Chinese
thing," remarked Gilbert with an injured air, "I
could call there to-night."

It is not by permitting mere sentiment to inter-
fere with work that literary men make their way.
This Gilbert knew. Therefore, at seven o'clock
that evening, Limehouse Causeway: Limehouse
Causeway guarded at the East India Dock Road
end by stout women in no hats, and oiled hair and
white aprons, to whom Lascars and Scandinavian
sailors threw words of raillery as they passed.
A scent of tarred goods and a scent of boiling
soup; at the door of a shop headed "Lew Ching
& Co.," three Chinamen arguing. At the
other end of the narrow street an ebony-faced
sailor, dancing for his own gratification a series of
intricate steps, creating no special interest on the
part of the occupants of doorsteps, but causing
much perturbation to the temper of a dirty white
little dog, who barked at the shining-faced
dancer and then ran away and barked excitedly,
as one demanding the police. On the window-

sill over Lew Ching's shop a bright scarlet counterpane fluttered; the scent of an uncommonly
good cigar, smoked by an unseen person, came
idly. Gilbert stood still and fixed the entire
picture on his mind. Then he entered the shop
of Lew Ching and made a trifling purchase and
looked carefully around. Lew Ching himself, a
yellow-faced, bony-cheeked celestial, in an incon-
gruous bowler hat and a drab cloak, smiled amia-
bly at his customer, and sold him a small pack of
Chinese playing cards at ten times the usual
price, with much geniality.

"What's the idea of this thing on the
counter?" asked Gilbert. He pointed to the
contrivance for counting.

"Make up figure," said Lew Ching; "count
lil money."

"And do you do pretty well?"

"Do vel ba'ly," complained the Chinaman.
"Sailor no coma see poor Lew Ching. Forget
poor Lew Ching. Ba' lot, sailor man. He no
good."

"That's a pity. And do you occupy all this
house?"

"How?"

Gilbert explained his question more precisely,

and Lew Ching in his loose-tongued English replied that he let his rooms. Lew Ching, looking narrowly at the inquisitive journalist, became suddenly reserved, fearing perhaps an approach to the subject of opium. Some one came down the stairs, and passing through the dark little shop spoke casually to Lew Ching and went on to the door. He stood there in the evening sunlight for a moment, and Gilbert looked at him.

"How do you do, Mr. Ford?" he said. "We meet again in an odd corner."

Mr. Ford (with no blue spectacles) came back into Lew Ching's shop, and failed for a moment, in the dim light, to recognize Gilbert.

"How do you know my name?" he demanded with some acerbity.

"Well, you gave me your card on the boat last night and——"

"I beg your pardon really." His manner changed at once. "I beg your pardon. You are the young journalist who was with—with——"

"Miss Reade."

"And you are here for copy?"

"That *was* the idea," said Gilbert.

"Do you know Chinese?"

"Heavens, no!"

"Perhaps I can help you, then." He spoke
again to Lew Ching, and Lew Ching bowed
respectfully. "I live over this shop. Come upstairs and I'll tell you any thing you want to
know."

"You're very kind."

"Oh, no, I'm not !" said Mr. Ford obstinately;
"I happen to be in the humor to talk. That's all."

Gilbert followed him up the rickety staircase
to the front room on the first floor. Mr. Ford
turned up the light of a red shaded lamp in the
corner, and Gilbert gave an involuntary excla-
mation of surprise. The room was handsomely
and quaintly furnished in the Chinese style ;
Gilbert had seen some photographs of interiors
at Hankow that were exactly similar. His host
sat on a rug and poured out some wine into a
long-stemmed glass.

"Are you afraid to drink ?" he asked.

"I think perhaps I'd rather not."

Mr. Ford laughed good-humoredly and stroked
the carpet on which he was sitting.

"You are cautious, Mr. Gilbert."

"It is a trait that I endeavor to cultivate.
'He was circumspect' is the epitaph that I have
written for my own mourning cards."

"It is not a bad idea," agreed Ford, "within certain limits. Tell me what you want to know of the Chinese quarter in London."

Fifteen minutes with the eccentric person seated on the yellow carpet placed the *Budget* youth in possession of all the facts that he required. As Ford became interested in his own descriptions the brusqueness of manner and the harshness of accent disappeared; in its place came a refinement of tone that Gilbert did not fail to notice.

"Tell me something now for my own personal information," asked Gilbert.

"Any thing that does not concern myself, I shall be——"

"But I am afraid it does. I want to know why——"

Ford held up his hand for silence. He took a cigarette from a brass lacquered bowl, and lighting it, looked up as the first puff of smoke wandered round the room in search of the window. Then he laughed a queer, short laugh.

"Decidedly I am in an odd humor this evening. I am going to tell you—*you* whom I met only yesterday—more than I have told any one else in the world."

He paused and Gilbert nodded.

"But," he went on quickly, "I am not going to tell you much. You will have to fill in the details for yourself, mind. All that I am going to tell you is that I am not one man but"—he coughed—"but ten!"

He looked at Gilbert to see the effect of this statement. Gilbert inclined his head, and remarked politely that ten was a good round number.

"Ten different and distinct persons," cried Ford, holding up the fingers of his hands; "ten! In the course of this current year I have already assumed three of these. A student of foreign life near the docks is No. 8 on the list. No. 9 on the list is—no! There is no necessity to trouble you with that."

"Is the student of foreign life near the docks about to relinquish his existence?"

"I think he has two days longer to exist," answered Ford.

"And do you like the life—I mean the lives?"

"Of course I do. What a particularly stupid question to ask!"

"It wasn't very intelligent," confessed Gilbert.

"Have you never felt tired of the hideous

monotony of the ordinary career of men ? Have
you never considered with horror the picture of
life with the same eternal person at the opposite
end of the breakfast-table each morning, the
same work at the same office, the same calls on
the same people—and all this to go on for the
rest of your existence. My God ! why is it
people don't scream out against this persistent
repetition of events?"

"I know," said Gilbert.

" Tell me, then."

" Because they like it."

Ford dropped the end of his cigarette into
another brass bowl, and stroked his clean-shaven
chin. A change came into his eyes, and they
twinkled.

"I suppose, then, you mean to suggest,"
he said good-temperedly, "that I am a little
mad."

"All intelligent men are," said Gilbert.

" Then I'm mad in a devilishly new and amusing way. You must confess that. I am trying
to enjoy life as much as——"

" Ten men ? "

" Yes ! " Mr. Ford rose to his feet and patted
Gilbert's back approvingly. " That's just it.

When I was only one man I used to have serious thoughts of suicide."

" And now ? "

" Why, now, I commit suicide whenever I have a mind to. To-morrow night, in all probability, the student of foreign life near the docks will cease for a year to exist. Very well, then. What happens is this : There is a new lodger in furnished apartments in Park Place, St. James's; a military man, who reads the service papers and has his own idea about Lord Wolseley."

" Does he live long ? "

" His," said Ford with candor, "is not a long existence. The moment that he is bored "—he gave an expressive wave of the hand—" out he goes."

" It's a perfectly delightful idea," said Gilbert. Then he added, " for those who like it."

" These cigars came from Cuba," said Ford. " Take one. And tell me six words about yourself. About your future. Only give me the outline, or you will weary me."

" I shall marry a lady named Miss Katherine Reade——"

" Whom I met yesterday. She is entirely charming."

"I shall scheme and contrive and do all I can to become a successful man. I believe many young men lose a good deal of the best time of their life by a too careful consideration of others and by a want of push. I have made up my mind not to let those considerations bar me. It happens that I am in an especially fortunate position."

"It will be interesting to see how it turns out," said Mr. Ford. "Let me go down stairs first."

Gilbert nodded good-night to the drab-gowned Lew Ching, and Ford, without his hat, saw him up to the end of Limehouse Causeway.

"You must take care not to ride your principles too hard," he said. "They break down if you do, and the last hurdle finds you without a jump left in you. And, above all, stick close to Miss—Miss Reade."

"I mean to," said Gilbert.

"A sensible girl can often make her husband continue to be her sweetheart all his life. You won't go far wrong if you go through life with her. I have never called myself a judge of character, but I am one nevertheless. And if I run across you again, I shall ask you how the scheme progresses."

"Do," said Gilbert.

"You will get a tram from the corner down there to Bloomsbury through the Commercial Road. Good-night, and good luck to you."

"By the bye," said Gilbert. "Who were you in the first place before you multiplied yourself by ten?"

Mr. Ford frowned slightly.

"I was the son of a Scotch earl,—not, I regret to say, a Representative peer,—and I married an American lady whose father knew the last word about pigs. She died, and then I died, and——"

"Is this true?"

"Oh, dear, no!" said Mr. Ford pleasantly; "oh, no! It is not true. But you asked a question that you had no business to ask, and I was giving it an appropriate answer."

CHAPTER VIII

IT really seemed that the world was going very well with young Gilbert. The Proprietor of the *Budget*, over green Chartreuse after dinner, assured him that he was a youth in whom he (the Proprietor) was determined to take a special and a lively interest, and the Proprietor of the *Budget* was notoriously a man of generous impulse. This was a fact known to all England. When, for instance, during his racing craze, he won a big race with Liverno, he straightway gave to the jockey the successful Liverno as token of his content. When, again, during his music-hall craze, Little Toff one Saturday evening raised the roof of the hall—"literally raised it" the professional organs put in, but this was an exaggeration—with his new song, "We can't do without 'em," did he not go round to the back and present the Little Toff with a diamond ring of excellent value? Emphatically, the Proprietor of the *Budget* was a good man to have on your side.

Moreover, Mrs. Brentford had been as good as her word, and an easy-going editor had written in a kindly way to Gilbert at her request. Miss Kittie Reade being informed of this fact, and of his indebtedness to Mrs. Brentford, bit her lips and frowned her pretty eyebrows and went straightway to the gymnasium in Albany Street, where she punched the ball with such determination and vigor for near upon half an hour that she felt afterward the calmer for the exercise.

"I hope I haven't hurt her," said Kittie to herself, "much."

Gilbert, having done a hard morning's work in his rooms at Doughty Street, sat in his easy chair near the window and looked out upon Bloomsbury.

"I don't seem to earn any thing great at this odd work," he said; "but there's no harm in slogging away. And there's the *Budget* money—that's a fixed income, and there's my reserve fund and—well, I mustn't complain."

A scarlet-coated, scarlet-faced young soldier was walking up and down on the other side of the street, waiting for his belated sweetheart. The soldier tapped his leg impatiently with his cane.

"And," continued Gilbert, "I am a precious deal better off in every way than I was at this age in my former life. The dearest possible girl is in herself enough to make one feel a millionnaire. Just to think of her eyes is to think of countless wealth." He hooked her photograph to him with a convenient golf-club and kissed it. "The dearest possible," he said.

The title had only been arrived at after some hours of consideration. It had made Kittie flush with pleasure when he had first called her by it, and a week's use had endeared it to them both. But they were careful not to use it in the chilling atmosphere of publicity—an atmosphere that always contrives to make terms of endearment appear wholly idiotic.

"Here's a bessedger with a letter, Bister Gilbert," said Ermyntrude at the doorway, "ad he's a-waitidg for ad adser."

"Another offer of the *Times* editorship, I suppose," said Gilbert with a bored air.

"Do they wadt you to be editor of the *Tibes*, sir?"

"They won't take no for an answer, Ermyntrude. That's what *I* complain of."

"What a duisadce!" said the small servant.

Gilbert scribbled a line on a correspondence card and enclosed it in an envelope.

"Let the lad take that to Mrs. Brentford," he said.

Gilbert, in shining hat and admirable frock-coat, looked at himself in the Psyche mirror in his bedroom with satisfaction. Mrs. Brentford had asked him in her note to come with her to the Botanical Gardens that afternoon, and Gilbert felt that it was an occasion deserving of some special attention in regard to his habit.

For he recognized that Mrs. Brentford was not only a smart and an acceptable and a genial person, but also one likely to be extremely useful. Wherefore, he smoothed his silk hat carefully.

"I think you had better be unusually cordial with her this afternoon," said Gilbert to his reflection in the mirror. "I am afraid that since the Thursday at Rosherville you have been a little reserved with Mrs. Brentford. As a cool, level-headed, sensible youth, Mr. Gilbert, it is your duty not to quarrel with all woman-kind just because you are engaged to one. There can be no harm, my dear chap, positively no harm, in keeping on excellent terms with Mrs. Brentford."

The scarlet-faced young soldier on the opposite side of the street was growing apoplectic in his impatience. He took the handkerchief from his sleeve and mopped his forehead. His lips moved as though he were making a remark to himself.

" 'Ello ! " said a voice, " 'ello ! Beed 'ere lo'g ? "

The short, belated maid crossed the road with an air of perfect assurance, adjusting the red sash on her white dress and patting her back hair.

"I don't know what you call long," growled the scarlet-faced soldier. "I seem to 'a' been 'ere the best part of a week."

Ermyntrude looked up at him.

"Well," she said calmly, "give us a kiss, at ady rate."

The scarlet-faced young soldier bent himself into the form of an upside-down L and did as he was told. Immediately his spirits returned and they marched off in the best of tempers. . Gilbert was much amused at the victory of the small servant.

"That's the result of strategy and impudence," he exclaimed. "*Savoir faire* is the only virtue that one really wants."

He took a hansom down to Queen's Gate, as being in accord with his appearance, and the page showed him into the drawing-room, where he waited in the well-furnished apartment. Perhaps some of the articles in the room were rather heavy in appearance, but that was reassuring in an age of insecure tables and unreliable chairs. On the table was a miniature, which Gilbert guessed to be a portrait of the departed Mr. Brentford.

"It is quite odd that I should find you looking at that," said Mrs. Brentford. There was always a suggestion of regret in her tone when she spoke of her husband, and nearly half a sigh. "For some reason I have been thinking of him a good deal."

"I seem to know the face."

"I don't think that is possible. I had not met you until after I—I lost him." Mrs. Brentford sighed. "Until he had gone to that bourn from which no traveller ever returns."

"If a traveller ever does return," said Gilbert, "he keeps the account of his journey very quiet. Are we ready?"

The Gardens were at their best and brightest. A Personage was expected,—an Eastern Personage,—and a band was stationed on an improvised platform near the large, white-faced conservatory, playing acceptable selections from the latest go-as-you-please musical comedy. To avoid the crowd, Gilbert and Mrs. Brentford walked along the red-gravelled paths to the ornamental water. The scent from the flowers and trees came lazily; and away, when the band ceased playing, they could hear faintly the sibilant sound of women's voices.

"You mustn't thank me, Mr. Gilbert, for any thing that I have been able to do. It gives me so much pleasure that I'm afraid it becomes purely a selfish act."

"I wish I could do something to show how grateful I am," said Gilbert.

"Really?"

"I should like to do some good work and bring it to you and say——"

"Your Christian name is Gilbert?"

"Yes, Mrs. Brentford."

"It is an odd name," she said thoughtfully; "Gilbert Gilbert."

"The fact is," said Gilbert, "*I* had no voice in the matter. That was the name chosen for me."

"So that it really doesn't matter whether you are called by your Christian name or your surname?"

"*Cela m'est égal.*"

Mrs. Brentford drew two capital G's on the red gravel.

"Then," she said a little nervously, pointing to the first G, "I think I should like to call you by this name."

"There is no earthly reason," said Gilbert, flushing, "why you shouldn't."

"The only thing is that you mustn't forget, please, that my name is Gertrude. That is to say, when we're alone."

"I see. When we're playing our usual parts you will always remain Mrs. Brentford."

She took a rose from her belt and played with it nervously.

"Yes," she said with a sigh, "I shall always remain Mrs. Brentford."

"That question," said Gilbert gallantly—"that question rests with you for decision. But I expect you are much happier as you are. You are quite free——"

"When a woman is free, Gilbert," declared Mrs. Brentford, "she wants to be enslaved, and when she is enslaved she screams for liberty. What is that they are playing now?"

It was the Eastern Personage's National Anthem, and they hurried from their seats to see him. The well-dressed mob had already penned in the Eastern Personage with so much complete-ness that they could only see his silk hat; and this, although a good silk hat and a shiny, failed to excite enthusiasm among most of those on the outside of the crowd. There were, however, exceptions.

"By gad, Louisa, this is a sight that makes one feel the greatness of England. Here's this Johnny come from the West to see the sights of the grand old country; and he'll go back to India, which I—er—once described rather well, I think, as the—er—brightest jewel in the—— Hullo, young Gilbert. How are you? Allow me."

Captain Dann presented Mrs. Dann, a lady of a bleached look, with much *empressement*, and then lifted his hat with so much grace to Mrs. Brent-ford that Gilbert was forced to introduce him.

"We're old chums, madam," said Captain Dann boisterously, "my young friend Gilbert and I. I dare say he has told you of rather a good thing that I recommended——"

"I did hear of that, Captain Dann."

"But our young friend here was too cautious; too cautious by half. Perhaps another time——"

"You must let me know if there's any thing else going," said Gilbert anxiously.

"There was not much encouragement," said Captain Dann, "in your conduct in that last affair. If I trust a man, I expect him to trust me. Isn't that so, Louisa?"

"Yes, dear," said the faded lady.

"I want confidence to be met by confidence, sir. That's me all the world over. But look here, I'll tell you what. We'll forget all about that business."

"Did the other man buy them?"

"Yes, confound him! And a devilish good thing he made over them. You ought to have had them, you know. I said to my wife—didn't I, Louisa?"

"Yes, dear."

"I said to my wife that night, I said, 'I would rather have *given* those things to Mr. Gilbert,' I said, 'than have sold them to that other bounder.' I believe those were my very words, Louisa?"

"Yes, dear."

"Look me up," said Captain Dann effusively,

"look me up at any time, and if you want a hint or two I'm not the sort to bear any ill will. Am I, Louisa?"

"No, dear."

"That was only one case of many, my boy," said Captain Dann. "Such chances crop up every day in the City. The great thing is to be on the spot, and to take instant advantage of them. Instant advantage, my dear sir; instant advantage. · Haven't I often said so, Louisa?"

"Yes, dear."

"There!" cried Captain Dann triumphantly, as though that proved every thing. "There! My wife has heard me say so."

Mrs. Brentford spoke to the monosyllabic lady, and Dann drew Gilbert apart.

"A wonderfully shrewd woman, my wife," said Captain Dann confidentially. "Wonderfully shrewd! An old head, as I often say about her, an old head on young shoulders."

Gilbert glanced at the reserved lady, and thought that the shoulders, too, were tolerably mature.

"I came across her first at a dance at Woolwich," went on Captain Dann. "She had a little money of her own, then, and in ten minutes I had made up my mind that she and no one else should be my wife. And I was attentive to her, and as true as I stand here, in less than a week—in less than seven days, sir—that woman had consented to be my wife. I've heard other people complain of their partners, but I've always found Louisa quite obedient. Quite obedient."

Gilbert remarked that marriage was always, to some extent, an experiment, and some were successful and some——

"The way I put it, my boy, is this : *I* always say that marriage is a lottery."

Captain Dann stepped back, the better to observe how Gilbert was affected by this novel and striking way of putting the matter.

"That puts the whole difficulty in a nutshell, Gilbert. Make a note of it, and keep it well in mind. An old stager like myself hasn't lived in this world all these years for nothing. Experience is the best schoolmaster."

Gilbert agreed. He felt that he had every reason to do so. But for his own store of knowledge of the world, he was quite sure he would commit blunders every day of his own life.

"I must give you a call again, Dann," he said.

"You know my address? Number a hundred and——"

The Eastern Personage came near them, and the clearance of the crowd enabled Gilbert and Mrs. Brentford to escape from Captain Dann's attention. They strolled off to chairs which they found under a large tree whose leaves afforded welcome shade.

"A queer fellow," said Gilbert, laughing; "but really there's something in him. I was a fool not to take his advice in regard to that Merry, Merry England affair."

"It is in money matters that I sometimes feel my loneliness," she said. "I get many invitations to speculate, and I want to be able to turn to somebody who has a man's knowledge of affairs and ask his advice. Do you see what I mean, Gilbert?"

"Well, Mrs. Brentford——"

"It is not well," she interrupted. "Have you so soon forgotten that my name is Gertrude?"

"I was going to say that if I can be of any use in that way I shall only be too glad."

It really seemed the least that the confident young man could say. Mrs. Brentford placed her hand lightly for a moment on his knee.

10

"You mustn't forget that promise," she said; "I shall bank it with any other promises that you give me—and some day—some day—I shall draw upon them."

"The check will be met—Gertrude." He smiled as he spoke. There is nothing quite so startling as the using of a *prénom* for the first time. "It's a good name, Gertrude," he added.

"It sounds good to hear you speak it."

The trees blurred oddly in the sight of the flattered youth; the white-faced conservatory danced an awkward but perfectly decorous *pas seul*. He held his breath for a moment and bit his lips. Then the gardens righted themselves, and behaved as though nothing had happened.

"Kittie!" he said to himself reproachfully, "Kittie, Kittie, Kittie!"

They had tea at four o'clock in Regent Street. In a corner of the restaurant was a correctly dressed man with a spiked, fair mustache. He held up a *Petit Journal pour Rire* in front of his face as soon as he saw Gilbert, as though he did not wish to be recognized. There were chattering French folk in the restaurant, too, and a few tired English girls, who had been to the Academy and apparently regretted it deeply. Their poor heads, they said, trying to fan themselves with the small, green-covered catalogues, were simply splitting.

"I like restaurants," remarked Gilbert. "Nearly every patron of a restaurant is a freak of Nature."

"You are a close observer," said Mrs. Brentford admiringly.

"It's copy," said Gilbert. He touched by accident the lady's small foot under the marble table, and she did not withdraw it.

"It must be delightful, Gilbert, to feel that all the world is offering you plots, and that you have only to pick and choose. Do you get an idea from every-body you meet?"

"Not every-body," said Gilbert importantly. It would have made a retiring youth feel conceited, this gracious interest, and Gilbert was not a retiring youth. "But now and again one strikes oil. I came across a good well a night or two since."

"Tell me."

Gilbert diverted Mrs. Brentford exceedingly by an exaggerated account of his visit to Lew Ching's shop and his encounter with the man of ten lives. An anecdote is much improved by artistic accentuation of points. The naked truth so frequently requires drapery.

"And I heard him as I came away," concluded Gilbert, "singing to himself a queer old tenor song. Imagine the situation. A dull, sleepy street; a single gas-light at the end, blowing gustily ; a sound of women using the language that is usual in Limehouse——"

"Dreadful ! "

"A roaring of wind from the river ; a good tenor voice singing."

"I am always fond of a tenor voice," remarked Mrs. Brentford thoughtfully. "When Mr. Brentford was alive——" She stopped and laughed. "That's rather like the conventional widow of the comic journals, isn't it ? I must be more careful."

"It is so easy," he said gently, "not to forget."

"Thank you, Gilbert." She leaned forward and touched lightly the hand that rested on the table. "You are the only person in the world who understands me. I wish sometimes that we had met earlier, so that——"

"I say," interrupted Gilbert, as he glanced at the clock, "I must get down to the *Budget*

office. Do you mind if I see you into a hansom?"

As they were leaving the restaurant, the
spiked-mustached man looked over the top of
the *Petit Journal pour Rire.* He watched the
two go through the doorway. He watched them
saying good-by, and he saw the swift look of
affection that Mrs. Brentford shot at the youth.
Then the well-dressed man with the mustache
looked at himself in the mirror and touched the
spiked ends and whistled softly.

"Well," said the military-looking man, folding
up the journal carefully, "I should never have
thought it possible. And he told me in Limehouse Causeway two nights ago that—— Waiter,
give me something to drink, d—— you!"

That evening at the *Budget* office Miss Kittie
Reade made her weekly call, and when Bradley
Webbe had left the office for a moment to find
Master Barling, she asked Gilbert what he had
been doing that day. Gilbert made answer that
he had been doing nothing particular, and he
kissed her on the lips.

"The dearest possible," he whispered affectionately.

CHAPTER IX

IT was partly with relief and partly with regret—but mainly, perhaps, with relief—that Gilbert heard, a day or two later, that Mrs. Brentford was leaving town for Coblentz. Mrs. Brentford had taken a dear little villa—it was her own description—a dear little villa looking over the Rhine Anlagen, and she proposed to stay there for a month or two. The agent had guaranteed it to be nearly covered with blue clematis, and the name, Villa Hermosa, could be altered for the time of occupancy if the temporary tenant so desired—most tenants, so the obliging agent said, had a preference for some special name ; a Scotch family who occupied it for a month last year had called the small villa Ben Nevis.

"You must be sure to come out for a week or two," wrote Mrs. Brentford. "A rest will do you good, and I shall have some bright folk staying with me. If the villa happens to be full, I can easily book rooms for you at one of the

Coblentz hotels facing the river. You will like
Coblentz. The German ladies, I am happy to
say, are all singularly plain, and they dress in
the fashion that was popular at the time of the
Crimea. You must call and say good-by to me
this week."

At Alpha Terrace that evening Gilbert mentioned the fact of Mrs. Brentford's approaching
departure to Kittie, and Kittie went straightway to the piano and played an air of special
joyousness.

"I wonder how many times a woman would
marry, if she had the chance, Gilbert?"

"Difficult to say, dear. The woman of
Samaria——"

She turned round on the music-stool with a
swish of her skirts.

"Do you like her?" she demanded.

"Who?"

"Mrs. Brentford."

"Oh, I don't know!" said Gilbert.

"Yes, you do, sir. Tell me!"

"Well," said Gilbert, "she tries to be
pleasant."

"Yes," said Kittie acutely, "I noticed that."

"But we needn't talk about her."

"Good gracious, no! There are many more agreeable topics."

"I want to speak to you about something. I have been asked to intercede with a lady on behalf of some one who cares for her a good deal, and I don't know quite whether to do it at all; or, if I do it, I am not sure *how* to do it."

"I thought it was only in short stories that men entrusted that task to other men," remarked Kittie.

"Oh, I am not empowered to make a proposal."

"That sounds more real."

"I am only to say words that shall soften the damsel's heart and make her contemplate my client with feelings of lively emotion."

"I don't like the idea of you going to a girl on that errand," said Kittie soberly. She rested on the arm of the easy chair in which Gilbert was sitting, and stroked his hair. "The girl is likely enough to say, 'Speak for yourself, John,' as she did in Longfellow."

"I think it quite likely," said Gilbert complacently.

"What size hat do you take, dear?"

Gilbert gave the information.

"I think you had better take a size larger. Your head is certainly swelling."

"Well, Kittie, it is of no use disguising the obvious, is it? I know very well that she is in love with me, and——"

"Tell me her name," said Kittie hotly, "and I'll box her ears."

"I wish you would. That's a promise, is it? I don't believe you'd dare to do it?"

"If she's as big as the side of a house," said Miss Kittie Reade definitely, "I'll do something to her."

"She's not so very tall. Just about your height."

"Good!"

"In fact, dear Kittie, you—you are the young person."

She stood up, flushing.

"Really?"

"On my honor."

She fanned her face with a sheet of drawing-paper.

"This is' romantic," she said, half-laughing. "I wonder who he is."

Gilbert told her, and Kittie Reade immediately became grave.

"Poor Mr. Webbe!" she said; "he's a good fellow."

"He's a better fellow than I am," said Gilbert honestly.

"He is always quite genuine."

"I don't know any man," said Gilbert, "for whom I have greater respect. He is not too brilliant, but he's a good worker, and some day——"

"He has been kind ever since I first began to do this fashion work."

"Bradley Webbe," said Gilbert, "is a straightforward, honest sort of fellow, with a great desire to be perfectly fair toward every-body with whom he has to deal."

"In fact," said Kittie, with a return to her usual brightness, "there is no reason why I shouldn't marry him, excepting that——"

"That?"

Kittie folded her arms, strode across the room, and spoke over her shoulder in the manner of ladies in melodrama.

"Sir," she said, in a deep voice, "I love a—nother!"

"Dearest girl!"

Mrs. Reade looked in at the doorway, and greeted Gilbert with great effusiveness.

"I'm sure," said Mrs. Reade joyously, "I was saying to Kittie only the other night how much we should miss Mr. Gilbert, if he left off calling, by any chance. Somehow, when any body becomes part and parcel——"

"We are just going out, mamma; Mr. Gilbert and I."

"Ah!" said Mrs. Reade bitterly, with her usual sudden change of manner, "there's a great deal too much going out with young girls of the present day. I remember when *I* was a girl I had to stay indoors and do crochet work or something useful. Not"—with much asperity—"not playing about with drawing new costumes of horrid girls with bicycles——"

"The work brings money."

"Money!" Mrs. Reade was very wrath at Kittie's reminder. "That's all some of you think about. Money, indeed! There are plenty of God's gifts in the world that will do you more good than money. What do *you* say, Mr. Gilbert?"

Gilbert answered warily that there was a good deal to be said on both sides. Kittie escaped to fetch her hat and coat.

"But you might as well talk to a deaf wall,"

said Mrs. Reade, with much acrimony, "as to try and knock a little sense into girls. *I* don't know what's come over them, really. I'm sure Kittie will go so far sometimes as to—actually to contradict me! Me, her own mother!"

Gilbert said soothingly that it was the tendency of the age.

"Bother the age!" exclaimed Mrs. Reade explosively. "I've got no patience with it. I wonder Parliament, or the County Council or something, doesn't step in with a firm hand and stop it."

Mrs. Reade fanned herself vigorously and compressed her lips tightly, as ladies do who dare not trust themselves to speak.

"But mind you, Mr. Gilbert," she said presently, "I wouldn't let any body else say a word against her. No! A better girl or a sweeter-tempered girl never lived. She can't do too much for her silly old mother. The way that dear girl nursed me when I was down with influenza I shall never forget. And you know, Mr. Gilbert, I'm not always the easiest person in the world to manage."

Gilbert was much astonished.

"No," said the old lady firmly, "I know my

faults; I'm not blind. We're none of us perfect, and——"

"The perfect woman," said Gilbert, "would be a perfect nuisance."

"Ah!" said Mrs. Reade, "how well you literary gentlemen put these things! I've often regretted that I never kept up my writing. When I went to school up at Hampstead—a good many years ago now—I used to write the most beautiful essays on 'How I spent my holidays,' and 'Love for animals,' and 'How to be happy,' and what not. Miss Robertson, the writing-mistress, used to say that I wrote a better hand than——"

Kittie appeared.

"Ready?" she asked.

"Quite," said Gilbert.

"I'm going to one or two shops in Bond Street, dear, to see some new costumes, and I shall lunch at the club. You won't be lonely until I come back?"

She kissed the old lady with an affectionate manner that seemed to Gilbert's eyes to take away immediately every suspicion of the ridiculous that had been present.

In Old Bond Street the two said good-by.

"Don't forget me, Gilbert," said the young lady.

"I never, never shall," said the young gentleman fervently.

At the Piccadilly end of Old Bond Street, Gilbert, walking along in his youthful, impetuous manner, avoided only by dexterity a collision with the Proprietor of the *Budget.* The Proprietor was beautifully dressed, as became a man of money; his necktie alone was a liberal education to the young. He was looking into the window of an expensive shop, apparently with a view of seeing whether he could find a new outlet for his money.

"You're looking extremely well, sir."

The Proprietor had been fearing that morning that he was looking out of sorts, and Gilbert could not have made a more diplomatic remark. There are some who delight to extol their complaints and make much of them: these are jealous of the introduction of any other topic, and do not greatly care to talk of the House of Lords, excepting as an opening to their favorite subject. The Proprietor belonged to the class who affect never to be in any thing but the rudest health.

"Never better, my boy," he said, "ne-ver better. But you—you are not looking quite up to the mark. Why not take a holiday? A short one, eh?"

"Bradley Webbe is away for a few days."

"Well, when he comes back, *you* go. And, by the bye, speaking of Bradley Webbe reminds me. I want to talk to you about him. He's a very good chap, and does the work well and turns out a very good paper, I admit, but—— Have you lunched?"

Gilbert had not lunched. The Proprietor took Gilbert's arm, and they walked together across Piccadilly to St. James's Street. As Gilbert ascended the steps of the Proprietor's club his feet were inclined to dance with satisfaction.

"They give you a devilish poor lunch here," said the Proprietor apologetically; "but perhaps you won't mind making shift with it just for once in a way. I have to complain of one or two things in this—— Waiter!"

"Yes, sir."

"Why isn't that window open over there? How many times have I——"

"Beg pardon, sir; it is open."

"Well, then," said the Proprietor, unappeased, "go and shut it at once."

"Certainly, sir."

"A more woollen-headed set of men than these club waiters I never saw; they've got no more sense than——"

Gilbert suggested with respect that perhaps they had to deal with some rather trying people.

"I'd like to try them," said the Proprietor humorously. "I'd give them six months' hard labor."

The sub-editor of the *Budget* laughed very much at this remark, and the Proprietor's amiability increased. The bottle of Chablis with the fish, the magnum of Perrier Jouët with the *entrées*, the liqueur at the end—all helped to increase the cordiality of his manner. The Proprietor was a man of sudden and intense friendships.

"No, no, *no*, waiter! These are not the cigars I want. You know that very well."

"Do you want those at one and six each, sir?"

"Good God, man! *I* don't care what they cost. Don't bother me with your confounded figures." The Proprietor glanced round at Gilbert for a look of approval. "Bring what I've asked for at once, and don't waste my valuable time."

The worried waiter brought a small pile of boxes, and the Proprietor with immense circumspection made his choice.

"Give this gentleman a light, waiter; can't you see he wants one?"

Gilbert sat well back in the exceedingly easy leathern chair placed in the bow window. He stretched out his long legs and gazed down into St. James's Street with kindly tolerance. Really it was, with all its faults, a very agreeable world. Very agreeable indeed.

"When does Bradley Webbe come back, Mr. Gilbert?"

"At the end of the week, sir."

"Oh!"

The Proprietor sent a ring of smoke up in the direction of the oak ceiling.

"What do you get now, Mr. Gilbert?"

Gilbert named the sum.

"Three hundred, eh? You're worth more than that, you know."

The youth flushed and said, laughing nervously, that it was impossible for him to controvert the statement.

"You're a very young man, certainly, for an editorship, but this is an age of renowned young men. Do you think you could edit a journal?"

There is no adult man in England at the present moment of writing—not one man—who would answer this question in the negative. Gilbert, for his part, said with much readiness that he would like a chance of trying.

"At six hundred a year?"

"The charge of the Six Hundred," said the delighted Gilbert, "is a capital selection. But what paper could I go for? There is no vacancy, is there?"

"We'll make a vacancy."

"On what paper, sir."

"Why, on *my* paper. On *my* paper. On the *Budget*."

"And get rid of Bradley Webbe?" gasped the sub-editor.

"Certainly—certainly! Why not?"

"Well, but," stammered Gilbert, "why should you? He does the work very well."

"I have no fault to find with the way in which he does his work, but—well, I've taken a dislike to red-headed men, and Bradley Webbe is red-haired."

"Still," urged Gilbert, "even a man with blue hair might make a good editor, if, in other respects, he——"

"Look here, Mr. Gilbert. We don't want to take up too much time over this matter. I'll tell you plainly what I want you to do. I'm a great man for having every thing done in a strictly business-like way, and I'll tell you exactly what my proposal is. I want you to write a letter to me, offering certain suggestions for the improvement of the paper."

"Right!"

"Then I want you to go on to say that there are one or two weak points in the present editing —lay stress on this, mind—and finally, say that if I decide to make any change may you offer yourself for the position."

The Proprietor waited.

"You see," said Gilbert slowly, "Bradley Webbe is a friend of mine. It looks rather like a mean attempt to oust him——"

"Mr. Gilbert! I'm a slightly older man than you. *Slightly* older, I say. And I can tell you that, if you're going to be so confoundedly punctilious in matters of business, you'll pass the last days of your life in the Scotch whiskey bar in

Milford Lane. You're an ambitious young man, and I want to help you. If you decline to let me assist you up one or two rungs of the ladder of Fame, why"—the Proprietor gave a gesture of despair—"it's of no use my troubling."

"Can I have a day to think it over, sir?"

"No!" Curtly and with much decision.

Gilbert rose from his chair and looked for a moment down at the street. Correctly-habited men were strolling along ; an open carriage with two Princesses drove down the middle of the street, and the shining silk hats went off. A man in a dust-coat stepped into a hansom and told the man to drive to the Horse Guards. It was all so much more opulent and attractive than Doughty Street, Bloomsbury.

"I agree," said Gilbert without looking round.

"Good!" exclaimed the Proprietor. "Let me have the letter to-day."

"You shall have it to-day."

"And make it hot for Bradley Webbe."

"I'll make it—make it hot for Bradley Webbe."

"Spoken like a sensible man of business! Which way are you going?"

"I am going to the *Budget* office first, to do some work——"

"And write the letter ?"

"Ye-es. And write the letter. And then I have to go to the City to attend a Company meeting."

"Shareholder?"

"Director," said Gilbert proudly. "A friend of mine, Captain Dann, introduced me to the affair. I am to get two guineas for every meeting, and I think the affair is likely to run through pretty well."

"Glad to hear you are making money. You'll find it a great assistance to you. And in regard to the *Budget*, Mr. Gilbert, rely upon me. *I'll* see you're safe there. You and I together will do big things."

"I hope so," said Gilbert soberly.

The prospective editor had written the communication at the *Budget* office (it was a task, to do him justice, of some difficulty), and had despatched it, when Barling, with a look of unusual moodiness, brought a post letter which had been placed in the wrong letter-box. Gilbert, desperately anxious to force himself into light-heartedness, asked Master Barling concerning the lady of Master Barling's heart.

"Oh, she's 'imiable enough," said Barling

gloomily, "just for the present. 'Ow long it 'll last, 'Eaven only knows. *I* don't. It's my belief that some people ain't 'appy unless they're a-breaking of honest 'earts."

"Still," urged Gilbert, "you're on good terms now."

"That's nothing to go by, sir," said Master Barling,—the small boy spoke as one who has drunk deeply from the cup of bitter experience, —"*that's* nothing to go by. I've never been particular 'appy in my life without directly after something 'appening to give me the 'ump."

"That's not an encouraging experience, Barling."

"And then she wonders that I ain't bright and cheerful and light-'earted! I'll defy any body to be reely bright and cheerful and light-'earted in this world. Some of 'em may pretend to be; but it's only a 'ollow marsk that they wear. You take it from me, sir!"

"I can't help thinking, Barling, that you adopt a somewhat pessimistic view of things. You must buy a pair of rose-colored spectacles."

Master Barling rubbed his chin with his grimy hand, and gave it a hue of blackness.

"I don't want no spectacles, sir," he said.

"I see too much of the world as it is. You cawn't trust any body. A chap calls 'imself your friend, and 'e's jest the one to go and take the very bread out——"

"It's the way of the world, Barling—the way of the world."

"It's 'igh time, sir, then, that it learned better. Any thing else, sir?"

"Nothing else, Barling."

The letter was from Bradley Webbe. Gilbert opened it with a sensation of hesitancy and reluctance that he had not, in his new life, hitherto experienced.

"MY DEAR GILBERT:

"Things have turned out badly here, and I might well have saved myself the trouble of coming down. For a reason that you, dear chap, will understand, I am bitterly disappointed.

"Fortunately, the excellent *Budget* is faithful. On the strength of that I shall try my luck as soon as I return. I have thought of her continuously. If I am successful, I shall owe much of my happiness to you, and I shall never forget your kindness. It is every thing to possess a good friend.

"I shall be in the Strand on Saturday to take up work again. If you think of going away, you might be prepared to start in the following week.

" My sincerest regards.

" Affectionately yours,

" F. BRADLEY WEBBE."

CHAPTER X

QUEEN VICTORIA STREET, City, on a bright summer afternoon, offers every attraction but shade. Queen Victoria Street commences near to the river-side, at a point where folk hurry toward the stone steps of Blackfriars Bridge, to take boat to Chelsea, and thence—for love of a roving life is a thing that grows on one—thence to Kew. Queen Victoria Street is not one of those streets which are unable to make up their minds as to the direction they shall take. It aims ambitiously at the Mansion House; and the directness and persistency with which it makes for that goal is a standing lesson to embryo Lord Mayors for all time. It is a busy street, too, much occupied with a variety of occupations; from huge iron machines, revolving ceaselessly for no apparent motive, to the College of Heralds, where the newest knight gets the oldest ancestry that his wife desires; from American typewriters to gorgeous outfitters where one may buy neckties that shall amaze suburbs and force them into admiration.

"Ah, Mr. Gilbert!" Captain Dann patted Gilbert's shoulders with both hands as he greeted him. It was a habit that some of Captain Dann's acquaintances did not care for. "That's right. Nothing like being up to time. It's an old saying of mine, you know, that time, to a certain extent, is—er—money. That's the way I put it, and by gad, sir" (frankly), "there's something in it."

"How long will the meeting last?"

"Well." Captain Dann whistled on the edge of his *pince-nez*. The *pince-nez* was a new adornment with the effusive gentleman, and with it had come a white hat and a tendency to frown. Generally, he seemed to wear a garment of prosperity that he had not hitherto put on. "Well, I should say an hour would cover it. I must introduce you to the other directors. And I say!"

Gilbert waited.

"I got them to elect you on the board, old chap, because I told them that you not only had a little money yourself, but you knew people who had a lot."

"I only know——"

"And, moreover, I told them that you had an

immense influence over the press of this country. That was what really fetched them."

"But I don't know that I could use the *Budget* in that way, Dann. You see it's a particular journal."

"It's just the particular journals that we want. You needn't puff the Company in a brazen-faced manner. All you have to do is to mention casually, at the proper time, that this looks like a big thing; that men with heads on their shoulders are managing it, and that the .shares will shortly go up by leaps and bounds, and——"

" But will they?"

Captain Dann whispered behind his large, fat, beringed hand.

" They will, my boy, if you say so. Besides, there's some news in store."

He pawed Gilbert again on the shoulder and took his arm.

"Got a cigar?" he asked, as they were going up the lift.

"Yes. Do you want to smoke?"

"No," said Dann. "But just light one, and then, when you go in the room, throw it carelessly into the fire-place. It will have a good effect."

"Pity to waste it, surely," said Gilbert, as he lighted a Manilla.

"It won't be wasted, my boy. Little actions like these tell strangers what a man is really like. There's nothing in this world like making a good first impression. I've known people—— Here we are. I dare say some of the directors have already arrived."

The smaller office of the Hip Hip Hurrah Mining Co. was a room with a green, baize-covered table in the centre and a sufficient number of chairs; on the walls maps of South. Africa, colored red and blue, with a large cross in one place. On the table lay sheets of white foolscap, and sheets of virgin blotting paper, and new pens and shining inkstands; all offering facilities to directors anxious to earn their fees by taking voluminous notes. A large, round, padded chair for the Chairman, at the head of the table; at the other end sat Mr. Matcham, with (seemingly) rather less chin than usual; his small eyes intent on a financial newspaper. Two or three men were talking in a corner.

"Matcham!" cried Captain Dann, as he brought Gilbert forward, "here's my old true,

tried, and trusted friend, Mr. Gilbert. You remember meeting a week or two since, you two?
I think I told you, Mr. Gilbert, that Matcham had
been appointed secretary of this company?"

"It's a devil of a tie," complained Mr.
Matcham. "I'm here till half-past four and
five o'clock sometimes."

"In the morning?" asked Gilbert sympathetically.

"Oh, no; in the evening. But the continual
grind tells on one, don't you know. I'm not
used to it."

"You soon will be," exclaimed Captain Dann;
"you'll soon settle down."

"Yes. I know," said Matcham despondently,
"in my grave. I've heard of people working
themselves to death before now, and I'm beginning to think——"

"Let me make you known to some of your
co-directors, Gilbert. Come along."

Mr. Blenkinsop. Mr. Percy Blenkinsop was
nephew of the Chairman (explained Captain
Dann), Jasper Blenkinsop, M. P. Good family
(whispered Captain Dann), devilish good family,
but deucedly hard up. Deucedly hard up, to be
sure.

"How do?" said Mr. Percy Blenkinsop languidly. "Strornary weather—time—year. What?"

Commander Harvey. Commander Harvey, bluff naval man with carefully trimmed black side-whiskers, hands ever in trousers pockets, and a suggestion of a lurch in his walk, as of one still at sea. Commander Harvey withdrew one hand from his trousers pocket and smacked with it the hand offered by Gilbert, much in the way affected by emotional leading men in stirring melodrama.

And the Hon. George Beauclerc. The Hon. George, a little perturbed by the arrival of Gilbert, inasmuch as he was thus interrupted in a humorous story at the very moment where the laugh should have come. The Hon. George prided himself on being a *raconteur;* he knew seven anecdotes, and they all had a strong feminine interest.

"Absolutely," whispered Captain Dann audibly—"abso—lutely *the* most amusing dog that ever came into the City."

"Oh, hang it, Dann!" protested the Hon. George.

"Come, now," demanded Dann boisterously,

"confess it. Confess it. Is it a fact or is it not a fact, that you, my dear sir, have a joke ready for every possible occasion? Have you ever found yourself nonplussed? Eh? Have you ever found yourself at a loss for a humorous remark? Eh?"

"Well," agreed the Hon. George frankly, "I must say I'm about as fly as the rest of them. Talking about being fly, though, reminds me of a girl at the Gaiety, and she——"

"The Chairman!"

The Chairman: a little late, but only because to be late was a busy, important, conspicuous thing to do. Mr. Jasper Blenkinsop bowed to Gilbert, sank into the chair, and looked round the table with the wearied, patronizing look of a statesman who is giving up his life to the service of his country. Captain Dann, seated by his side, whispered the word, "Minutes."

"The Secretary," said the Chairman sonorously—"the Secretary will be so good as to read the minutes of the last meeting."

Mr. Matcham, screwing up his small eyes, read hurriedly the minutes of the last meeting.

"Those who are in favor of the minutes being signed as correct will signify——"

"I don't wish to delay this meeting," interrupted the burly naval gentleman, "but we want everything straight and above-board. Those minutes say that Mr. Percy Blenkinsop moved that a further call of five shillings per share be made. Now I want to point out to you, because, as a naval man, I believe in having the thing done correctly, that *I* moved that resolution. *I* did it. *I* spoke to it. *I* was asked to move it, and *I* moved it."

Commander Harvey, very red, leaned back and tapped the table nervously with his fingers, as one who has felt it necessary to clear his character from lasting dishonor.

"What's the use of talking like that?" asked Mr. Matcham from the end of the table. "Here it is, down in black and white, and how——"

Captain Dann had whispered again to the Chair.

"You will make the necessary correction, Mr. Secretary," said the Chair severely.

It was the Speaker's style of sitting on recalcitrant members in the House of Commons, and Mr. Jasper Blenkinsop flattered himself that it was not a bad imitation. In fact, if any thing were to happen to the Speaker, it was obvious, in

Mr. Blenkinsop's opinion, that no one was so well qualified to take the place as himself.

"You will excuse me reminding you, sir," whispered Captain Dann respectfully.

"Certainly, Dann; certainly. I've got a marvellous memory," said the Chair, "but now and again it wants jogging. It's the constant wear and tear in the House that takes it out of a man."

The Chairman rose, a sign that he was about to address the directors on a subject of importance.

"Mr. Speaker, sir, in asking the House—I beg pardon, I beg pardon. Gentlemen, excuse the slight slip of the tongue. I have to speak to you on rather an important question. Mr. Matcham, is the door closed?"

Mr. Matcham—with a sigh intended to convey a remonstrance against the laborious nature of the new undertaking which he was requested to engage upon—went over to the door ; opened it and closed it carefully.

"I hope, gentlemen, you will take careful note of what I am about to say. It appears that a cablegram will shortly reach this country——"

"Hear, hear!" approvingly from Captain Dann.

"Which will give—shall I say an encouraging account—yes, a *most* encouraging account of the Hip Hip Hurrah Mines. You are aware that these mines have not for some time past held a favorable position in the estimation of the public. The one-pound shares, now fully paid up, are quoted at an absurdly low figure."

"Hear, hear!" regretfully from Captain Dann.

"Gentlemen, it is not we who are responsible for much of this. When the old directorate resigned we took the helm of the ship and led it forward—if you will excuse the metaphor—across the field of battle, strewn with bodies of like companies, in the hope of finding the promised land. Like the Egyptians of old——"

"Hear, hear!" reverentially from Captain Dann.

"Like the Egyptians of old—like the Egyptians of old, we——"

The recollection of the Chair did not appear to be able to take him into the details of that remote period.

"At any rate, it is time we made something out of this concern. We came in cheap, gentlemen, we shall go out dear. The spoils to the victor."

"Good!" cried Captain Dann enthusiastically. "Spoils to the victor! Good!"

"This cablegram will be communicated to the newspapers on Tuesday morning next. To-day is Thursday. My advice to you all is, then, to buy carefully any Hip Hip Hurrah shares that you can. On Tuesday and Wednesday next I venture to think that you will be able to dispose of them at excellent prices."

"Excuse me," said Gilbert, "but how do we know that the cable will arrive?"

The Chair rose excitedly. "I am not, gentlemen, in the habit of finding my word doubted——"

"I am not doubting your word," persisted Gilbert hotly. "You have not yet given it."

The Chair looked despairingly at Captain Dann, as who should say, "This is what comes of letting in outsiders."

"Seems me," said Mr. Percy Blenkinsop, with much effort, "seems me—something in what Mr. I-forget-his-darn-name—er says."

"If we know that a good find has been made, then, I think," went on the new director, flushing, "that we ought to make the news known to the shareholders. If we don't know that a good find has been made, how can we be sure that we shall know on Tuesday next?"

Gilbert had not stated his argument quite so clearly as he could have wished, but he hoped he had made it sufficiently obvious.

"I don't want to make any trouble," went on Gilbert, with less heat, "but at the same time I don't want to get into any trouble. At present it looks as though——"

"Allow me," interrupted Captain Dann. "Perhaps a few words from me will clear the air. A stitch in time, as I often say, saves as many as nine, and if I tell my dear friend Mr. Gilbert that I stake my reputation on the arrival of this cablegram before Tuesday morning next; that I'll forfeit my head—my head, sir, on the block, if it does not arrive; why, then I feel sure that he will agree with every word that you, sir, have said. I may remind my young friend Mr. Gilbert—one of the best and brightest and cleverest journalists of the day, gentlemen, and one for whose name on the scroll of Fame a bright space is waiting—I may remind him that on a former occasion he omitted to take my advice——"

"I agree," said Gilbert, abashed.

"My idea is," said the Hon. George, "that

our motto's this:' Keep your eye on Cap'n Dann
and *he* will pull you through."

General agreement. Commander Harvey half
inclined to take his hands out of his trousers
pockets and hail the Chairman, but not seeing
exactly what he should say, determining after
consideration not to do so.

"Gentlemen, you honor me." Captain Dann
flourished his red silk handkerchief and dabbed
his eyes with it. "You honor me. I am proud
of your confidence—I say it frankly. I am not
one of those who are ashamed to acknowledge
that they are trusted by honest men. Give me
(as I have said on more occasions than one) give
me the man of an—er—honest heart. Gentlemen, thank you."

There was some further business, but Gilbert
sat back rather sulkily and did not trouble to
listen. Instead, he thought of Kittie, and he
thought of the *Budget*, and he thought of many
things that had no reference to the Hip Hip
Hurrah Mining Company.

"Then you agree, gentlemen," said the Chairman, "to take this important step. It seems
to be the only thing we can do, and our friend,
Captain Dann, says that we are safe in doing it."

"The law can't touch us," said Captain Dann.

Still more business, engineered mainly by the excellent Dann, and Gilbert's admiration for that gentleman increased as he noted the tact with which he managed every one around the table. When the Hon. George Beauclerc interrupted with a devilish good story that a Stock Exchange man had told him, it was Dann who sidled round to the Hon. George and listened attentively, and prevented the recital from delaying business. When Mr. Percy Blenkinsop could not find his eye-glass, it was Dann who scribbled a line, "It is on your back," and passed it along to the distressed youth. When a question arose of the time a steamer would take from Cape Town to Southampton, and Commander Harvey grunted and growled at the clumsy guesses of the land-lubbers, it was Dann who said, "Gentlemen, pardon me for interrupting, but we are favored with the presence of a colleague whose knowledge of the ocean is limited only by the bounds placed on it by the possessions of our great country. Will that gentleman—need I say that I refer to Commander Harvey—will he decide this question for us?" And his deference to the Chair, and the way in which, while apparently conceding to that difficult gentleman, he always managed to make the Chair do exactly what he wanted the Chair to do, was in itself a generous education.

"Gentlemen," said the Chair, "a most satisfactory meeting! Most satisfactory! I promised the Whips that I would be back in the House by five-thirty; where my vote is required on a subject to which I will not, with your permission, further allude."

Cheers from Captain Dann, indicative of commendation of the politician's diplomatic attitude of reserve.

"Thanks to the attention which you have given to the business of the Hip Hip Hurrah Company" (the Chair glanced at his nephew's blotting-pad, whereon that languid youth had depicted an extremely plump young lady in tights), "I have been able to stay to the finish. May I say that just as our motto is 'aspire,' so should we hope that now the clouds are rolling away from this undertaking to which we have the honor to belong; that the clouds will be washed away by the—the sudden wave of prosperity——"

"Capital!" murmured Captain Dann. "Wave of prosperity. Capital! capital!"

"Wave of prosperity which I see in my mind's eye, no bigger, perhaps, than a man's hand, but destined, as I hope, to grow, to accumulate, to increase, to enlargen—if I may use the word—until the bright sun of joy once again rains down upon us its generous gifts."

The Chair put on his hat and found his stick, and seemed half inclined to weep. There were, indeed, tears in his eyes as he waved good-by, and, with the haste of a man who feels that the political world is waiting impatiently for him, hurried away.

In the outer office Gilbert waited a few moments. Four or five clerks were doing a little work, and doing it with much assiduity. They all frowned at their books and at their correspondence, and they bit their lips as though the concentration of intellect were doing them a serious injury. In the corner a telephone with a junior clerk speaking at it. Gilbert looked at the telephone and smiled. It reminded him of an incident in Cheyne Gardens only a few weeks since,—it seemed like several years,—and he wondered what these people would say if he were to tell them the facts. He felt that it would be useless to do this, even if he were so inclined. In his case nothing would sound quite so untrue as the truth.

"Oh, and I say, Miss——"

The junior clerk was unaware of the presence of a director, and was giving a little exhibition of mannishness for the benefit of the other clerks. He was a small, brush-haired boy, and he had to stand on tiptoe to speak.

"And I say, Miss, what are you doing next Sunday, eh? You don't know? Well, what do you say to Kew? You say 'no fear,' do you? All right then, don't! I dare say there's plenty of other girls——"

A cough from one of the seniors caused the junior to look round, and he stopped at once.

"That telephone is on the Central, I suppose?" asked Gilbert.

. "Yes, sir."

"So that you can communicate to almost anywhere?"

"Yes, sir."

Gilbert stood looking at the instrument, and the senior clerk waited respectfully.

"Wonderfully ingenious invention, sir," remarked the senior clerk. "Quite in its infancy, too, they tell me."

"I suppose so," said Gilbert absently.

"If you had told people thirty years ago that the time would come when they could speak to each other from London to Paris, why, they would have stared like any thing."

"That would have been the least they could do."

"Quite so, sir. And of course they've become a great convenience; I don't know what we should do without them now; do you, sir?"

"No," said Gilbert, "I don't."

Captain Dann's hand fell upon his shoulder.

"One moment," said Captain Dann. "Just step this way, Mr. Gilbert." They walked to the corridor. "Be very careful not to let that little matter of the coming telegram slip out. What passes in a Board Room is of course in the nature of—er—what I call a Cabinet secret. You'll be very careful, won't you? In next week's *Budget* you can boom the news for all it's worth."

"I should like to let a friend of mine into the know," said Gilbert.

"One friend?"

"Only one!"

"Personal friend?"

"Yes, certainly, a personal friend; some one who has been very kind——"

"If you can trust your friend, Mr. Gilbert, well and good. But *do* be careful. These little things so easily go wrong."

Gilbert went down the lift. Outside, in the bright sunlight of busy Queen Victoria Street, he stopped.

"I'll go straight to her," he said.

He hailed a hansom and stood on the step to speak to the driver.

"Queen's Gate !" he said.

CHAPTER XI

THE Rhine in August belongs not to Germany, but to America and—in a lesser extent—to England. The *Kaiser Wilhelm*, the *Germania*, and the other awning-covered steamers that hurry from Cologne to Mayence, are boarded by folk speaking either the English or the American language; the hotels that give their titles in three languages, so that none may have cause for hesitation, are in a state of siege, and nobody relishes the invasion more than the invaded Germans. Mr. Gilbert—journalist, financial man, engaged youth, one with the rosiest of prospects—had stood at the side of the steamer as it left Cologne and had laughed with satisfaction. His reception at the Coblentz landing-stage by the entire household of the Villa Hermosa was most gratifying; but not more gratifying than the attentions that were paid to him during the week. Rooms had been taken for him at the Hôtel du Géant, and his days were spent in trips organized by the assiduous Mrs.

Brentford. The party had been across the river
to Ehrenbreitstein—with the exception of the
stout youth, Mr. Lancing, who objected to all
exercise as cruel; they had been down the winding, undecided Moselle to Trèves; they had
been up the Rhine to Bingen; they had held
a picnic near Stoltenfels. *Aucun incident*, as the
French journals say. But Miss Campbelltown,
of the *Ladies' Own*, had told the stout minor
artist (whom she loved) that something was
going to happen soon.

" Mark my words," Miss Campbelltown had
said mysteriously.

They were sitting on one of the balconies on
the Rhine side of the Villa Hermosa. There
were many balconies at the Villa Hermosa; a
distinct advantage, inasmuch as if you wanted
to evade old Howson, who had been an editor
of some paper in the fifties (now extinct), and
cherished against somebody a grievance that was
at least forty years old, you went to the upper
balcony, where you perhaps found little Miss
Howson, his daughter, whose company was the
more gracious; similarly, if the lady of the house
desired to consult Gilbert on financial matters—
Mrs. Brentford insisted on looking upon Gilbert

as a prospective governor of the Bank of England—why, there was sure to be a disengaged balcony overlooking the Mainzer Chaussée.

"I am sorry to be so near the end," said Gilbert.

He rested an elbow on the wooden railing of the balcony, and took his cigar-case from his pocket. In doing so a letter in the familiar writing of Kittie Reade fluttered down, and, as he picked it up, he flushed.

"The regret will be mainly on my side," declared Gertrude Brentford earnestly. "*Do* smoke."

"I suppose, when I get back to the *Budget*, I shall have to take off my coat and do my best to fill Bradley Webbe's place." He laughed a little uneasily. "Poor old Bradley Webbe! He's unlucky."

"Why is he leaving?"

"Well, I scarcely know how to explain it. The Proprietor didn't care for him."

"Of course, Bradley Webbe can't say that you have helped to oust him out of the position?"

"I *hope* he won't say that," answered Gilbert with some anxiety.

"He is sure not to hint that you have done any thing unfair," said Mrs. Brentford. "Any one who knows you, Gilbert——"

"Quite so, quite so."

"Would never think of suggesting that you could act in any way——"

"I suppose that is so."

"Ah!" said Gertrude Brentford, "you have all a good man's modesty."

Gilbert picked a flower from the creeping blue clematis on the wall, and hummed a tune softly to give himself time to regain his self-possession.

"I wonder what your future will be like, Gilbert?"

"I beg your pardon?"

Gertrude Brentford repeated the question. She leaned back in the basket chair and placed one small foot on a ledge of the balcony. It was a small, neatly-slippered foot, and there was thus every excuse for giving it some little prominence. Too often it is the large, bulging, elastic-side boot that is allowed by ladies to be *en évidence;* boots which bring no gratification to the heart of man, and should be used exclusively for the purpose of frightening birds. The silver buckle on Gertrude Brentford's slippers caught the last rays of the declining sun through the lime-trees and made Gilbert blink as he glanced at it.

"It's rather difficult to say," answered Gilbert. "My future depends, I suppose, partly on myself, partly on my friends. In some moods I foresee Westminster Abbey; in other moods the pauper side of Kensal Green. Can you do any thing at palmistry?"

"Not unless you give me your hand," she said softly.

The voice of Miss Campbelltown came from the small drawing-room below. Miss Campbelltown was a good journalist, but, as little Miss Howson remarked, she could not sing for nuts. Now, not to be able to sing for nuts is (one may translate for the benefit of country gentlemen) to sing with want of accuracy. Gilbert had only half heard the last remark and did not reply.

"Let us go out into the avenue," said Mrs. Brentford. He picked up a lace shawl and placed it over her head. "Thank you so much."

It was growing dim out in the long, long avenue that reaches from the barracks at Coblentz up to Laubach. Here and there statues of Fame and of Liberty, and other abstract things, gleamed at the side; a few hard-up German officers were strolling along, wooing, with military pertinacity, plain daughters of well-to-do Coblentz tradesfolk.

"Do you mind taking my arm, Gilbert? I am afraid of stumbling. Let us walk in this direction; we can find a place to look down upon the Rhine."

"I admire the Rhine too much to do that."

"I want to ask you something. I want to ask you if you—if you are engaged."

There was a pause.

"Well," said Gilbert evasively, "I have no contract signed with the Proprietor, but if he gives me the editorship, I shall insist——"

"Are you engaged to Miss Reade?"

"To Miss Reade?" He coughed. "Oh, no!"

It is so easy sometimes not to tell the truth. People say the thing untrue either because they are lazy, or because they are ingenious. As a matter of fact, Gilbert blurted out this denial mainly because he did not want to have to enter into explanations.

"I am *so* glad. *So* glad. She is a good, dear little girl, but——"

"I admire her very much," remarked Gilbert earnestly.

13

"But she is not quite the wife that you want. She will make somebody very happy, but——"

"It's a pity that these things are not managed by a State department. It would save people a great deal of trouble."

"I suppose some people like the trouble. Here is the place."

They could look across over the low, solid brick wall at the broad river. By the side of the wall was a map of the Rhine from Cologne to Basle. The birds, looking down upon the two, twittered in the high branches of the trees with an air of lively interest, as who should say, "Here's more fun." It occurred to Gilbert quite suddenly that Gertrude Brentford was an exceedingly good-looking woman; the faint suspicion of matronliness that day-time with its brutal frankness suggested was absent now.

"I suppose that being in love," she said slowly, "is a kind of agreeable madness."

"I believe that marriage not infrequently restores the patients to sanity."

She turned to him quickly.

"Why do you always talk like that, Gilbert? You make me think at times that you are wanting in sincerity. It is because you are trying to conceal your real self !"

" I am always rather cautious, I suppose. The fact is that, before my present life, I had the experience of forty years. That enables me, you see, to avoid the errors other youths commit."

"You absurd person !" laughed Gertrude Brentford. The quaint conceit restored her good humor, and she patted his arm with an affectionate manner of reproof. "One cannot be annoyed with you."

"But touching this question of wives," said Gilbert.

It is not easy to say why, at this moment, Gilbert placed his hand gently on her shoulder. Gertrude Brentford gave a little shiver of delight and did not protest.

"What kind of a partner do you think I ought to advertise for?" he went on.

"I think," she said slowly, "that you want some one whose position in the world would help you. You want some one who can take a sincere interest in all that you do. You want some one who—who loves you. You want some one who can help you at once to make a name in the world. You want——"

"It's a long advertisement," interrupted Gilbert. He touched a vagrant curl on her neck, and as he bent his head slightly the soft perfume of her hair came to him. "And there would probably be no answers."

Her fingers played a quick tune on the low brick wall.

"There would be one answer," she said slowly.

"From whom?"

She stepped back suddenly, and held out her hands to him appealingly. The birds up in the branches sang with much excitement.

"Can't you see," she cried with something of a wail in her voice—"can't you see that I love you?"

The birds up in the high branches of the limes of the Rhine Anlagen twittered now with enthusiasm, as though the sight of two mortals holding each other in their arms for a brief moment were the most gratifying spectacle in the world. Gilbert had not hesitated; he saw, with the foresight that experience gave him, in a quick flash of anticipation the advantages of a wife with a house in Queen's Gate. Years of his new existence would be economized; at one step he would be able to breathe an atmosphere of luxury.

He kissed Gertrude Brentford on the lips, and the excited birds flew off to tell other birds of their acquaintance all about it.

"You mean that?" he asked. "You mean that you *do* love me? I want to hear you say it again."

"I am willing to say it all my life," she answered softly.

"I wonder—I wonder how it is that I have never guessed this?"

"Perhaps it was because you were not——"

"Not conceited enough? That was it. I never dared to think for one moment that you would care to marry me; I should never have ventured to ask you."

"The fact that I proposed to you, Gilbert," she said nervously, "is not to be remembered to my debit."

"They say the queen did it," answered Gilbert encouragingly. "As a loyal subject, the least you could do was to emulate her example."

"But, Gilbert," rather anxiously.

"Gertrude."

"You—you have always cared for me, haven't you?"

"Since the moment that I first saw you," said Gilbert gravely.

He comforted himself with a swift reflection that the moderate form of the question enabled him to answer it with absolute truth. And No. 310 Queen's Gate was really a charming house; his study would look out on the Institute.

He took her arm, and they walked down the long, foliage-roofed avenue toward the villa.

"I wonder what would happen," she asked laughingly, "if a woman were to propose to some one who didn't want to marry her."

"Quite easy, dear. The gentleman would reply, with becoming modesty, that it was impossible to give the hand where the heart could never be, and he would offer as an alternative to be as a brother to the lady."

"There is really no reason why men should claim the monopoly."

"It is a relic of the barbarous age," agreed Gilbert. "We are working away from the old practice of permitting the gentleman to stun the lady with a battle-axe and ride off with her, but the process is slow. Do you mind doing something to oblige me, Gertrude?"

"With pleasure, dear."

" Kiss me again."

Decidedly Gilbert's experience came to his aid effectively now, for he showed none of the *gaucherie* that the average youth exhibits in trying circumstances. Gertrude Brentford, sincerely happy, stood at the tall iron gate leading to the garden of the Villa Hermosa.

" We must come out here next year, Gilbert," she said contentedly. " You will be host then, and you must invite your friends."

He took her chin and looked into her eyes.

" Would you like me to tell these people now ? " he asked; " or shall we keep it locked in our own hearts as a mysterious secret ? "

" I think—I think I would rather it were known to them. Besides, they will be sure to guess. Is that a steamer going down ? "

Out on the Rhine the *Germania* was making its way back to Cologne, pushing along with much determination, and making the river form miniature affrighted waves. A baritone voice came from the deck through the still air, singing:

> " Ich habe ja Ew'ge Treu verspochen dir,
> Wohl unter heissen Wonneküssen.
> In meinen Augen siehst du mehr
> Als Mond und Sterne wissen."

There was a pause.

"'In meinen Augen siehst du mehr,'" echoed Gertrude Brentford softly.

There were tears in her eyes.

"Gilbert Gilbert," said the young man to himself, "you are a scoundrel. You are behaving like a scoundrel, and you *are* a scoundrel."

Nevertheless, he managed to enter the drawing-room of the villa with some gayety of heart. He could see so well that it meant prosperity, and the thought soothed his indignation at his act. It is easy to persuade ourselves that we are not really so black as in a moment of anger we have painted ourselves; one must use tolerance in this world, even in regard to our own faults.

"Miss Howson, come here; Miss Campbell-town, come here also, please. I want to speak to you on a subject of importance."

"Good Heavens, Gilbert!" said old Mr. Howson, "you are not going to propose to both of them, are you?"

Old Mr. Howson laughed so much at his joke that he coughed and was forced to sip his whiskey-and-water.

"I scent romance," said the stout artist

lazily. "I find a distinct suggestion of romance.
I hope it will be understood that, while I am not
unwilling to listen to romance if it comes to me,
I am willing to make no effort to go out to meet
romance."

"Where is Mrs. Brentford?" asked Miss
Campbelltown.

"She is gathering a buttonhole in the garden
for me."

"Is there some hidden mystery here?" demanded old Mr. Howson, chuckling. "I
remember at the time of the Crimean war—I
was a mere youngster at the time—and a lady
of my acquaintance——"

"I only want to tell you," interrupted Gilbert,
"that Mrs. Brentford has promised to be my
wife."

Mouvement. Gertrude Brentford, entering,
was immediately kissed by the ladies and
covered with exuberant congratulations. The
servant bringing in wine, old Mr. Howson
craned himself into a standing position, and
offered his good wishes in a little speech.

"Young people : this announcement fills me,
and I am sure every one else, with the greatest
delight. I have known our charming hostess for

some time; I knew her poor husband, who was certainly the oddest——"

Miss Howson coughed warningly.

"I'm sure that you'll both be very happy. My friend Gilbert, if he will permit me to call him so, is one of those men who are bound to get along in the world. The stars in their courses fight in his favor——"

"Hear, hear!" from the stout artist.

"And, if our good wishes are of any effect, he will be very, very happy with his delightful companion. Journalists nowadays have opportunities that in my younger days were never dreamed of. In '55, as I may have mentioned to one or two of you, I was unfortunate enough to encounter the most confounded scamp of a——"

Little Miss Howson coughed warningly again.

"Let me conclude by asking you all to drink to their healths and to their great prosperity in a good, honest, English way. Ladies and gentlemen, charge your glasses. Mrs. Brentford and Gilbert, to you!"

Gilbert, rather nervous, begged to be allowed to say, very briefly, thank you. If he had been an orator, he would have bored them with a speech.

As it was he could only say again for his dear love—

Gertrude Brentford's eyes fill again.

—And himself, thank you, and good-night.

"My dear Mrs. Brentford," said Miss Camp-belltown, "I knew it all the time. And I'm *so* pleased, really."

Miss Campbelltown was eliciting additional facts, like the practised interviewer she was, by a visit to Gertrude Brentford's room.

"And may I mention it, when I return, in the *Ladies' Own?* I can make rather a charming little par. out of it."

"Please don't. I am not sure that Gilbert would care for it to be publicly known yet."

She stood up in front of the cheval glass and looked contentedly at the reflection of a glad face.

"You look five years younger, dear Mrs. Brentford," said the lady journalist ingratiatingly. "I must really see about falling in love myself, if it has that effect."

"I am so very happy," said Gertrude Brentford softly, "that I think presently I shall cry."

Miss Campbelltown, having promised to keep

the additional details an absolute secret, looked
in at Ethel Howson's room on her way to her
own bedroom and confided the new information
to that young person.

"Good !" cried little Miss Howson. She
turned down the page of her novel and closed
it, for love in real life is so much more interesting than love in books. "I am glad to hear it.
I could see she was fond of him."

"I don't see that that has any thing to do with
it," grumbled Miss Campbelltown. "I wonder
how many times she expects to marry. There's
little chance for us single girls, if widows are to
go on like this. Surely a maximum of one ought
to be fixed."

"Have you never been engaged, dear ?"

"Well, I *have* been engaged," said Miss
Campbelltown guardedly, "and I *haven't* been
engaged, if you can understand that. Some
men are very careful not to absolutely pledge
their word to you. Besides it's a well-known
fact that folk don't marry so frequently nowadays as they used to."

"I shouldn't want to marry frequently," said
little Miss Howson, nursing her knees. "Once
would do."

"What I mean to say is that it's a distinctive thing for a girl to do to remain single all her life."

"It might be distinctive," said little Miss Howson. "It would certainly be very disappointing."

CHAPTER XII

IN his room at the Hotel—facing the bridge of boats, facing the Rhine running swiftly Cologne way, facing the high fortress of Ehrenbreitstein, which keeps a frowning eye on both the Moselle and on the sturdier and more decided river—in his room a clever young writer was in the throes of composition. There are several dodges at the disposal of literary men to enable them to write, and they select the one which affords them the greatest assistance. Some walk about their study for a space before applying themselves to work, much as though they were engaged on a go-as-you-please race, and when they finish the last lap they seat themselves and write quickly. Others, of whom in a general way Gilbert was one, dispense with this pedestrian exercise and let the pen do as it pleases, correcting the pen's errors afterward. In the work upon which Gilbert found himself engaged, neither plan seemed of much assistance.

"My Dear Kittie:

"My short holiday is nearly over and I shall be back at the *Budget* early next week. I dare say that we shall see each other.

"I have been considering our engagement and——"

There it seemed his powers of composition ended. The ink had long been dry, and the various ways of continuing the letter were confusing themselves in his brain.

"It is not easy," he said thoughtfully, "to play the part of a scamp, but——"

A steamer with cargo was coming up the Rhine. Two boats of the bridge, creaking and grumbling bitterly at being disturbed so late at night, came away with grudging politeness and allowed the cargo-steamer to pass through. There was some severe *badinage* in German; the two boats went back and took their place in the bridge. Down below, at the tables outside the restaurant next door, was a queer, foreshortened view of white-topped tables and fierce-mustached officers in uniform, and long, thin glasses of beer. A couple of privates stopped in the roadway, and saluted, with much

care and particularity, the seated, fierce-mustached officers.

"But," said Gilbert to himself, "it's of course
the best thing to do for every-body. And "—he
tried to laugh and failed—"and especially for me."

He looked out again at the river; looked
across the river at the high, burly fort; tried
hard to listen to the talk of the people below,
and saw *not* the Rhine and Ehrenbreitstein,
heard *not* the talk of the people below, but saw
Kittie Reade taking up the letter which he was
trying to write from her breakfast-table. Saw
her kiss it and hide it in her blouse. Heard
old Mrs. Reade's distracting conversation. Saw
Kittie at the earliest opportunity take the letter
from its sweet resting-place, open the envelope
with much care (for lovers' letters, mind you,
are not to be torn open roughly as though they
were circulars from the draper), saw her open
the letter and read the first lines. Saw Kittie's
face go white; saw the blouse palpitating hurriedly; heard her scream——

"I'm upsetting myself for nothing at all,"
cried Gilbert, wiping the perspiration from his
forehead. "It's quite .likely that—that——
Where's my pipe?"

If a man likes to smoke, and if a man flatters a certain tobacco by remaining constant to it, that tobacco will repay his devotion at certain crises of the man's life in a most valuable way. Before Gilbert's pipe was half done he had finished his letter. He sat back when the task was over, feeling somehow more content than before. This slight revulsion of feeling increased until he approached the stage where men wonder with a kind of gratified surprise at the very moderate character of their vices. If he had been the average sentimental youth, he would have clung to his first promise, and Queen's Gate would have weighed as nothing; being (he argued) a young man of considerable experience, he had seen in a moment which was the most profitable course to pursue.

He took up the letter:

"MY DEAR KITTIE :

"My short holiday is nearly over and I shall be back at the *Budget* early next week. I dare say that we shall see each other.

"I have been considering our brief engagement, and I want you to let me say honestly what I think of the matter. I hope you will

14

believe that I like you very much. But we are both young, and I think we became engaged without due and sober consideration. Shall we cancel the past, and see at the end of twelve months whether we care for each other well enough to resume the engagement?

"I like to think that you are a common-sense little woman, who will look at the whole affair as calmly as I do. Let me know what you decide when I return.

"Meanwhile and always,

"Believe me,

"Yours sincerely,

"GILBERT."

Gilbert read this through several times, and dotted the *i*'s, and inserted commas with particular care. He sighed.

"Now," he said, "if any one will kindly come and knock me down several times I shall feel better."

He addressed the envelope. By force of habit he placed on the flap of the envelope the tiny cross which Kittie and he had always placed on their communications. He addressed another, and rang the bell.

"Sare !"

"I want you to get me a twenty-five pfennig stamp, waiter."

"In two minutes, sare."

The waiter reappeared with the stamp, and stood while Gilbert slowly placed it on the letter.

"Lods of beople in Coblentz," remarked the waiter. "Ver' busy. Many Am—ericans haf gome here alretty."

"Post that," said Gilbert after a pause, "and come back here."

A gleam of satisfaction came over the waiter's face as he glanced at the address.

"Goot !"

When the waiter returned, Gilbert was sitting on the ledge of the window. The waiter was a tall, middle-aged man with domino-shaped whiskers and close-cut hair. As he looked up to touch the lamp, the light fell distinctly on his face.

"Why, I know you !" cried Gilbert quickly.

"Possible, sare."

The waiter turned away, as though anxious to avoid recognition.

"Why, you—you are——"

"I've never been discovered before," said the

waiter, laughing. He sat on the table with easy, well-bred familiarity. "Don't let any body know, that's all. You're a sharp fellow, Gilbert, to recognize me."

"What number of life is this?" asked Gilbert. The diversion of encountering Ford came opportunely, for his thoughts were not entirely pleasant.

"Well, this is a new life altogether," said Mr. Ford. "Adopted for a special purpose."

"Which is?"

"Which is," said Mr. Ford, "a secret."

"What a man you are!"

"I am several men. I have only arrived today, and I shall stay a week. But I shall be particularly obliged, Mr. Gilbert, if you will take care not to speak of me to any body. I have a very urgent reason for that."

"Rely upon me."

"And if I can do any thing while I am here, to assist you in any way, I shall be glad."

"You can do something for me at once. Bring some whiskey and some mineral water in those cool little jars, and two glasses——"

"Two?"

"Yes," said Gilbert; "one for yourself."

When Ford brought the glasses he sat down
and allowed Gilbert to play the host. The hour
was late, and his services were not required elsewhere in the hotel.

"When did I see you last, Mr. Ford? I don't
think I've seen you since I visited Limehouse
Causeway."

"Really?"

"But I have wondered once or twice what you
were doing. I thought your next life was to be
a military person, with rooms in——"

"He's buried—for the present. I came to
Coblentz because——"

He hesitated, and pushed his chair back into
the shade.

"Because my wife is here."

"You married? And what in the world does
your wife think of your eccentric behavior?"

"She does not mind," answered Ford calmly.

"That's lucky for you. Some wives would
seriously object to having so many husbands. Is
she staying in lodgings in the town? I should
like to meet her, and see what she thinks of you."

"You shall," said Mr. Ford, in the shade, "if
it is convenient. I am going out to North Africa
next week."

"Another quick change! And do you take her with you?"

"Good God, no!" exclaimed Ford. "I can only endure the society of men for a little while; the society of women sends me frantic."

"With joy?"

"No, no! with annoyance."

"You ought never to have married, Ford."

"I know that," said Mr. Ford, "now. It was a great blunder of mine. Unfortunately, it is one of the few blunders that cannot be remedied without an infinite amount of trouble."

"But I fancied you rather enjoyed your present attitude of irresponsibility."

"Why, yes, I believe I do; I am sure I do. But I am not certain that some day I shall not tire of the monotony of change and begin to think about returning to the old life."

"Your wife will be pleased."

"You think she will, Gilbert?"

"There can be little doubt about that. What shall you do in North Africa?"

"My mind is not yet made up. I thought at first about being a missionary, but I saw portraits the other day of some, and——"

"You pass the missionary idea."

"Yes. I think I shall do some shooting."

"Take care that the natives don't ; they have an awkward habit of potting Europeans with their Birmingham rifles."

"Nothing would suit me better," said Mr. Ford cheerfully. "It would save me and other people a lot of worry. But I suppose it is a notorious fact that those who want to die can never do so."

"It's very hard," said Gilbert.

"Suicide is such a messy business. Besides, it always looks so theatrical."

"It's a drama that I don't care for," agreed Gilbert. "I think a man should endure his life, and let Providence say when it is to end. Providence knows best: it has had such a lot of experience."

Ford rose, lighted another cigarette, and, leaning his elbows on the mantle-piece, looked down at Gilbert. There was always a certain refinement on Ford's face, and his carefully-tended finger nails were in themselves almost enough to betray him.

"You're going back to town ?" he added abruptly.

"Yes ; I can't stay much longer."

"Going to get married soon, I suppose ?"

"As it happens, you are right, Ford. I *am* to
be married very soon. I have just been making
some arrangements this evening."

"I am pleased to hear it—very pleased indeed.
And look here, Gilbert: I don't know whether I
ever mentioned it, but—I have plenty of money."

"I guessed you were not a pauper."

"And on your wedding-day I wish you would
do me a favor. I shall be away a few thousand
miles at the time, and I should like to feel that I
was doing something to help to make you both
happy."

Gilbert rose, with genuine recognition of
Ford's generosity.

"I'll get you on the morning of the wedding
to send a letter down to Cox's, the bankers, asking them for a parcel addressed to you. In it
you will find some things of considerable money
value, which you and "—he smiled one of his rare
smiles—"young Mrs. Gilbert must please accept.
There, don't thank me; I am doing it for quite
a selfish purpose. It is only to afford myself
gratification."

"I am sure that it is exceedingly good of
you," cried Gilbert. "She will be delighted. I
shall tell her all about you——"

"Pardon me; no. I am sorry in a sense that you recognized me to-night. Don't talk of me, please, to any one else more than you can help. The satisfaction of the life would be gone, if I once felt that it was known to many people. Is she as old as you?"

"I rather fancy," said Gilbert, "that she is slightly older."

"Oh!"

"But—" hurriedly—"the difference is nothing to speak of. And, as there is no occasion to wait, I dare say we shall be married at once."

Mr. Ford walked to the window, and sat with his back to the river-side and his head bowed.

"I remember," he said slowly, "that when I was married I thought the world was going to reconstruct itself for my special convenience. I thought that I myself should be altered, and that it should be——"

"Roses, roses all the way," suggested Gilbert.

"Yes. And my wife was younger than I, and we were happy, and I was some one else until— No." He stopped suddenly. "No, I'm hanged if I'm going to become a bore! Mr. Gilbert, why didn't you stop me?"

"I was interested."

"All that I shall tell you is that it was my fault. Any ordinary man would have been exceedingly happy. Now, I am no ordinary man, unfortunately."

"That is true."

"All the same——"

"Well?"

"All the same, I'll have a little more whiskey-and-water, if you don't mind."

"My dear chap, why didn't you help yourself?"

"I do, generally."

Gilbert put in some whiskey, filled up his glass with water from the slim stone jar, and Ford took two drinks.

"I shall be sorry to say good-by to you," said Gilbert earnestly. "I have a feeling that something untoward is going to happen to me, and I should like to have a man like you to advise me. I have had a great deal of experience altogether, but I fancy you, with all your oddities, have a good fund of solid sense. Two heads are better than one."

"It depends on the quality. Twice one is two, but twice nought is nought."

"I am not prepared to disprove that calculation. But yours is a good head, and I—well, I wish we were not going to part."

"God bless you!" said Ford. "I shall think about you a good deal. We needn't say good-by now, though."

He went out, and Gilbert took off his coat. His bedroom was the next room, and he shied the coat through the open door on to the bed. The bed had a puffed, inflated little scarlet counterpane on the top, which seemed to be placed there in order that it might slip off during the night. Germans have a style of humor that is peculiarly their own.

"For a man," said Gilbert, swinging his arms as athletic young men do before retiring to bed—"for a man who has done an uncommonly base action I feel, on the whole, singularly comfortable. I suppose, after a time, it will become a positive source of delight."

Mr. Ford reappeared at the doorway. He took a *Pall Mall Gazette* from his pocket, and glanced at it.

"I found this down stairs, Mr. Gilbert. If you haven't seen a London newspaper for a day or two, you may care to have it."

He shook hands. At the door he stopped.

"Any ordairs for the morning, sare?" he asked deferentially.

"No, thank you, Fritz."

"Good-night."

The newspaper had a piece of late news inserted hurriedly in the "fudge," headed:

"NEWS AS WE GO TO PRESS

"Warrants have been granted against the directors of a well-known financial scheme. The Old Jewry authorities are taking steps for the immediate arrest of those concerned."

"Ah!" said Gilbert philosophically; "if people will dabble in shady matters, they must expect to be tripped up."

He glanced at the cricket scores.

"Well done, Grace!" he cried approvingly.

CHAPTER XIII

It was a heavy, close morning when Gilbert opened his window; there were gray-brown clouds above, and the sun had apparently given up the task of endeavoring to pierce them. A sound of grumbling came now and again from the skies. The youth at the window hastily attributed his vague feelings of depression to the atmosphere, and forced himself to ignore the fact that he had not been able to sleep until a late hour. The tiny book-stall leaning against the office on the side of the river was being arranged by its proprietor, and Gilbert observed that the proprietor opened and flattened out two London morning papers.

"Goot-morgen, sare," said Ford respectfully. "You dake goffee or tea, eh?"

"Coffee, Fritz."

"You sleep well, eh?"

"No, Fritz," said Gilbert. "I slept badly. I began to think; and to think, you know, is always fatal to a night's rest. Ask the head waiter, will you, where I can buy a good bouquet."

A few large spots of rain splashed lazily on the cobble-stones as Gilbert went out to the market in quest of flowers. The trams with a bright brass bell in front were running round the town from the Rhine to the Moselle Station, but he preferred to walk.

"I forgot to buy that *Daily Chronicle*," he exclaimed to himself. "I must get it when I return."

He looked at the board outside the *Coblenzer Zeitung* office, and felt surprised to find that the news blue-pencilled upon it was not of his engagement to Gertrude Brentford, but a mere everyday item announcing the assassination of a Bulgarian statesman. In the market he caused such intense commotion by demanding the best bouquet the crowded little space could furnish, that he ran some danger of being smothered by the offerings of enormous ladies, whose figures were rather more lumpy than the average sculptor conceives to belong to Flora. He pencilled on a card, "With *all* my love," and walking down the Mainzer Chaussée left the bouquet at the Villa Hermosa, with a message to the effect that he

would call again later. The voice of Miss Campbelltown, singing merrily as she descended the
staircase, made him hurry incontinently away.

"*I'm* going to have a bath," said Mr.
Ford.

He was in tweeds and was standing at the
entrance to the small *Bad* attached to the bridge
of boats on the Ehrenbreitstein side. It was
odd to notice how completely (despite the domi-
noes of black whiskers) the man was able to put
off the German waiter with the dress suit.

· "It is terribly close," he added.

"Good idea !" cried Gilbert. "I'll do the
same. I've walked to and from the Villa Hermosa, and——"

"You have been there this morning ? "

"A friend of mine, Mrs. Brentford, has rented
it for a month or two. I spend most of my time
there."

There was a roll of drums from the skies that
seemed almost to prepare one for a shrill march
from fifes.   ·

"Oh !" repeated Mr. Ford thoughtfully.
"You spend most of your time there. But
Miss—Miss Reade is not there, is she ? "

"Miss Reade," said Gilbert, with some fri-

gidity of manner—" Miss Reade, as a matter of
fact, is *not* there. Miss Reade is in town."

" Charming young person ! "

" Ye-es. Yes, she is. Oh, yes, certainly. I
should think she will marry very well some day.
She is clever, and she is——"

" But excuse me ! I understood that you were
engaged to her ?"

" Did you ?" said Gilbert airily. " There
must have been some mistake."

" Evidently," said Mr. Ford, with sudden
gravity of manner. " Will you wait for me, if you
come out first ? I want to speak to you on rather
an important subject. We can walk along this
side of the river and cross by the little steam-
boat. How long shall you be ?"

A good plunge into the delicious cold water
did Gilbert a great deal of good. After all, as he
argued with himself, after all one often feels a
sensation of impending evil, and the evil so rarely
arrives. He was to lunch at the Villa Hermosa
at one o'clock, and there would be the gratification of feeling that he was master in embryo of
the house; that next year, if he and Gertrude
were to come here, it would be his duty to assist
his agreeable wife in dispensing hospitalities.

He thought, as he rubbed himself into a ruddy condition and redressed, that it would be rather a kind thing for him to ask poor Bradley Webbe, and Gertrude could ask Kittie.

"Really," said Gilbert generously to the warped, undecided slip of looking-glass, "really, one ought to try to do *some* good in the world."

Mr. Ford was seated on the wooden rail of the bridge, swinging his stick in a thoughtful way and humming softly. He slipped down and took Gilbert's arm, and the two strolled on.

"Can you spare ten minutes, Mr. Gilbert?" he asked.

"Twenty."

"Ten will do. Perhaps two will do."

"The shortest stories are sometimes the best," said Gilbert, "if only there be incident enough."

"I am not sure whether there is enough incident to suit you. There is a Miss Campbell-town staying at the Villa Hermosa, I think."

"Journalist girl. Sings a good deal and always sings wrongly. Kind of girl who will make some man happy by not marrying him."

"And a Miss Howson."

"Not a bad little girl. Her father's a

15

bore, but we shall all be bores when we are old enough."

"And the others?"

"Well, there's a minor artist chap—more minor than artist, I think—who, if he only goes on increasing in size at the present rate of progress will, I think, eventually be able to make a very good income in another way. And old Howson, as I said, is a man with a grievance that has grown since its birth to such an extent that now it fills a room. Taken altogether, though, they are a very amusing set, and I—I enjoy myself there a good deal. Every-body is very attentive."

"And you? You are attentive to——"

"Myself," said Gilbert promptly.

"The only lady remaining is Mrs.—Mrs. Brentford."

"Yes," said Gilbert, flushing. (It is a tiresome habit of youth to flush at inconvenient moments. Even the gifted people who write "Answers to Correspondents" in the weekly journals are helpless, when asked for a remedy.) "Yes, Mrs. Brentford."

"Do you admire her?"

"Well," said Gilbert, "it's a very odd thing

you should ask that question. I admire her so much, and my good fortune is so great, that I—I am going to marry her."

There was a pause.

"Come, Ford! Congratulate me."

"I don't think I will," said Mr. Ford slowly. "Not just yet."

"Well, that's frank, anyway."

"I shall have to be even more frank than that, I fear. You know already a good deal more of my life—of my lives—than any one; I'm afraid I must tell you some more. I dare say you look upon me as a crank; as a man who is only removed by a few short steps from lunacy."

"On the contrary," declared Gilbert, "I am not sure that you are not the sanest man I ever met."

"Glad to hear you say that. I am a selfish man, I confess. I have always done the thing that gave me greatest satisfaction, and as I have always had plenty of money, there has been no good reason for changing my procedure. If I had had to earn my living, circumstances would have forced me into something like convention-ality."

"You may have your faults, but you are cer-

tainly not conventional. At least, not often.
I was amazed, though, to hear you say that you
were married. That was a terribly commonplace action. Such a lot of men do it."

"I am afraid it *was* a blunder. I saw that
soon afterward. It was a blunder for which, as
we were saying last night, I, and not my wife,
was wholly responsible. I could have remedied
the situation by dying, but——"

"That's the last thing that one thinks of doing."

"I suppose, despite what I sometimes say,
that I am rather fond of being alive. One knows
at any rate what *this* world is like. And I must
confess, although I have grumbled, that, by
taking a lot of trouble, I have managed to enjoy
life since fairly well. And now I must try to tell
you something that affects yourself."

"I don't think you can," said Gilbert airily.
"Is it any thing about the *Budget ?*"

"Nothing about the *Budget.*"

"Any thing wrong about the Hip Hip Hurrah
Company ?"

"A company with so exuberant a title could
scarcely, I should say, go wrong. The information I have to give you is of a more personal
nature."

He laid his hand on the young man's shoulder.

"Fire away!" said Gilbert.

"I told you that my wife was at Coblentz. I hinted that I did not want to see her, and that I was sure she did not want to see me. Now then, brace up, Gilbert."

He held Gilbert's arm somewhat tighter.

"My wife is Mrs. ˙Brent—— Don't stagger like that, man—Mrs. Brentford."

The great drops of rain again came languidly down from the heavy sky, and one splashed ludicrously on Gilbert's nose.

"Don't be a—a d—— fool!" he cried nervously.

"I'm not. I'm quite serious. I should never have told you, if it had not been that——"

"But her husband was drowned. She had a letter from the Consul at——"

"I know; I wrote it myself." Mr. Ford laughed oddly. "But it—it wasn't true. I can easily give you proofs of the truth of what I say."

The restaurant over the way danced a confused, preposterous dance in the eyes of Gilbert. He struck Ford stupidly on the shoulder, and Ford gripped him by the arm.

"You see, it is this way," explained Ford; "I should never have dreamed of interfering, had it not been——"

"Don't say another word," cried Gilbert hoarsely; "let me get back to the hotel and—and think."

They embarked on the small steamer and crossed the river. Gilbert stared steadily before him, endeavoring with no success to re-assort his thoughts, and neither of the two spoke. They had to wait while one of the Rhine steamers passed down to the pier where passengers embark for Cologne, and Gilbert chafed, with apparently no reason in the world, at the delay.

"Give me a paper," he said to the man at the small book-stall.

"Tib Bis?" asked the German book-stall man, offering a green-covered periodical.

"A newspaper, confound you! A London daily paper."

The man found a *Standard* and took thirty pfennigs for it, and Gilbert, cramming it into his pocket, strode across the roadway to the hotel. At the entrance he steadied himself and looked round.

"Did you post that letter last night?" he demanded brusquely.

"I bosted it," said Mr. Ford, in his most respectful German waiter manner. Another waiter was near. "I bosted it, sare, immediate that you to me handed it. It is nearly in London alretty."

Gilbert stumbled upstairs to his room and threw open wide the window. On the table was a square little envelope addressed in a firm, decided handwriting that was not unfamiliar. He was about to tear it up, when he stopped.

"I may as well see what she says, perhaps. Ford won't mind—if he doesn't know."

The letter inside had the monogram "G. B." in the corner, and the printed heading "Friday."

"An unlucky day," remarked Gilbert grimly.

"My Dearest Gilbert:

"Why did my dear boy not present his charming flowers in person? I was waiting to see you: waiting to hear you tell me that there *is* such a place as the Rhein Anlagen; that there *is* such a lover as Gilbert Gilbert; that it *is* true that Gertrude Brentford is the happiest woman on the Continent of Europe.

"Be punctual for lunch. I am too joyful to

write. I only want to see you and to hear your dear voice.

"Yours now and always,

"GERTRUDE."

Gilbert sat down in the low rocking-chair and laughed foolishly. He laughed until a catch came into his throat, and then he felt that if he had not been a man he would like to have cried.

He rang the bell.

"I say, Gilbert," Mr. Ford, in his waiter's dress again, closed the door carefully before he spoke—"I say, don't let this upset you, you know. I know, of course, that I am a good deal to blame, but you will see that I had no other course to pursue. Here is an old letter of hers I have brought to show you, and here is a photograph of our two selves taken at Neuchatel. And although I am most anxious not to be bothered, still, if you insist upon it, I will drive down to the Villa this afternoon, and——"

"I shall not go there again."

"Perhaps that would be the better plan. I'll write a note, if you like, to her that will explain every thing. Then I shall get down to Marseilles and cross over to Algiers."

"Your behavior is very rough upon her."

"I don't quite see that," said Ford, with a touch of obstinacy. "She has been a good deal happier than she would have been if I had stayed on. She has plenty of money, and unless she invests it stupidly——"

"I shall get back to town," interrupted Gilbert. "This place is like hell to me."

"It will be cooler than hell," said Ford, looking out of the window, "after the rain. And after all, you still have your excellent prospects, and in a little while you will have forgotten all about this."

"You're a queer kind of Enoch Arden, Ford."

"I'm afraid I am. What train are you going to catch?"

"The first."

"I'll go and get your bill. We shall both of us be much amused at this incident in the days to come."

"Possibly. Just now it seems to me to lack several of the cardinal elements of fun."

Gilbert packed his portmanteau and took up the *Standard*. He noticed with satisfaction that Surrey was doing well; that the batting averages

were keeping up, and the ground having been
rather dry, the crack bowlers had been able to
do very little. There is something marvellously
cheering to the average man in seeing a record
of centuries. Gilbert turned over the paper and
glanced at the police intelligence. A special
paragraph near to the column was headed:

"SERIOUS CHARGE AGAINST DIRECTORS

"The sitting Alderman at the Mansion House
will have an important case before him to-day.
The directors of the Hip Hip Hurrah Mines will
be charged on warrants with conspiring to
induce a post-office official to issue a forged
cablegram purporting to come from South
Africa. The proceedings have been taken
hastily for the reason that it was feared some
difficulty might arise in the serving of warrants.
As it is, two of the directors are abroad, and
they will probably remain there until the case
is decided.

"The Hip Hip Hurrah Company was formed
in——"

He looked hastily at the end of the paragraph.
A list of the directors was there given, and one

line seemed to stand out as though the words were being shrieked:

"Mr. Gilbert Gilbert, journalist, of 84 Doughty Street, Bloomsbury."

He went to the table, and with a trembling hand poured out a glass of water. When he had drained that, he found with difficulty—for the light in the room seemed strangely dim—a time-table. A train left the Moselle Station in twenty minutes ; and travelling by way of Trèves, Luxemburg, and Brussels he could reach Charing Cross at five-forty-five the following morning.

On his way down stairs he encountered Ford.

"I am going," he said thickly, "at once. At once. Write to her and explain. Pay the bill with this."

There was no one else on the landing, and Ford drew the agitated young man aside.

"You are doing quite the right thing," he said kindly. "I think I will call at the Villa this evening and see her. I hate a scene, especially where women are playing in it, but I must endure it—for once. Good luck to you!"

He took Gilbert's portmanteau with a change
of manner.

"The hotel 'bus," speaking loudly, "he go to
start di-rectly. Al-low me, if you blease."

Gilbert stepped into the 'bus. There were two
other passengers; an obviously new husband
and an obviously new wife, both in the best of
spirits.

"What a happy, happy place Coblentz is,
Reginald. I should think nobody was ever sad
here; should you, dear?"

The new husband looked nervously at Gilbert
and said that he supposed not.

"I shall always look upon Coblentz as a town
of joy," said the new wife enthusiastically.
"Whenever I see the word in print it will always
make me good-tempered. And if——"

"Don't talk so loudly, sweetest."

"My *dear* Reggie! I'm sure I wasn't talking
loudly. What a cross boy you are! You say
such unkind things sometimes——"

"Sweetest! I never mean them, if I do.
You are always the best and prettiest——"

The new husband patted the cheek of the new
wife. Gilbert looked out of the window, and
they kissed furtively.

"Naughty boy! My hat's all crooked now, I'm sure. Put it straight, you sad, sad scamp!"

The sad, sad scamp did as he was bid and received a mock-warning shake of the head from the new wife for his shocking behavior.

"Let me wave my hand to the Rhine, Reggie dear. Let me say—oh, now we're off."

The manager on the doorstep bent respectfully to the departing guests; Ford behind him waved his hand to Gilbert. A detachment of mounted soldiers cantered past; their accoutrements glistening, despite the absence of the sun. The giant drops of rain once more began to patter, striking the roof of the small, jolting omnibus with decided taps.

"Well," said the new wife contentedly, "it doesn't matter now if it does rain. It's been fine all through the honeymoon."

CHAPTER XIV

THE train pursued with ardor and pertinacity the elusive Moselle between Coblentz and Trèves, and Gilbert, by dint of persistently keeping his bare head at the open window, managed to divert his thoughts to some extent from the dire prospects that awaited him in London. To some extent only. Nothing could remove that leaden feeling of dismay that stuck somewhere just below his throat. Forcing itself steadily through the scene of a broad, winding river with vines growing in steps on the high, green hills beyond, came now and again, in the manner of a dissolving view entertainment, a scene of the little square Justice Room at the Mansion House, with sharp solicitors in frock-coats, a shuffling crowd at the back, kept in order by the precise, footman-like jailer, and on the high-backed chair beneath the sword, the queer old Alderman, cracking old jokes with a broad Scotch accent. This scene gave way to one at the Villa Hermosa with Mr. Brentford, otherwise Ford, explaining to Gertrude Brentford; and this in its turn faded, to be replaced by a picture of Kittie Reade opening the letter from Coblentz and shrieking.

Gilbert closed his eyes. He cared for this last picture the least of all.

"Will you 'low me to offer you a cracker," asked the white-haired American lady opposite.

She handed him a paper bag, and Gilbert took a cracker and thanked her politely. Her husband was asleep in the other corner, and her daughter, in a violet veil, was writing, as well as the movement of the train would permit, to— judging from the look upon her face—some lucky youth in the United States.

"Don't speak of it," said the old American lady volubly, "don't speak of it. I always think it passes the time 'long so much more pleasant to talk to your fellow-passengers. I can't sleep in the train."

"I also," said Gilbert wofully, "do not anticipate being able to sleep. I have a good deal to worry about."

"Come out of that!" said the old American lady cheerfully.

"I wish I could."

"Why, you've got every thing in your favor," she said. "You've on'y got to hustle."

"I've tried that," said poor Gilbert, "and it doesn't seem to answer."

"P'raps you ain't hustled enough."

"I'm afraid I have hustled a little too much. I've had a good deal of experience, and I've tried to use my knowledge of the world, but somehow or other——"

"It 'll dry straight, I shouldn't wonder," said the old lady.

"I don't see how it can. It's as crooked as it can be, now."

The daughter looked up, from under the violet veil folded just above her eyes, with some curiosity.

"Finished your letter to Peter Thornhill, Julie?"

Julie said No, Ma. She'd got such an awful lot to tell him, added Julie frankly.

"Engaged," whispered the old lady confidentially, "to as good a chap over in Chicargo as ever breathed the American air."

"Well done!" said Gilbert.

"She's a bit dif'cult to manage, though," went on the mother, still in a whisper. "It 'll be a rare good thing for Julie, you see, and the only way we can keep her up to the mark is by saying things agenst him."

"Against him?"

"Fact! It's only been necessary to say in Rome, f'r instance, 'There's goes a young fellow like Peter Thornhill—only better lookin',' and she'd flare up, bless you, Julie would, and go off and write a nice lovin' letter to Pete by the next mail. Our Chicargo girls are very independent, don't you see."

"It's a good thing—for them."

The father moved in his corner of the compartment, and put his large, white felt hat straight.

"In Chicargo, sir," he said, rubbing his eyes, "we have houses seventeen stories high, and a weather——"

"Go to sleep, Larry!"

And the father obediently went to sleep again.

The old lady's chatter certainly assisted to shorten the journey. She was an entertaining old lady, and she had been to the Tower of London, and to Stoke Pogis, and to Windsor, and to several other places which are names only to most Englishmen. When Gilbert obtained

16

fruit for her at Namur, and a huge thick slab of gingerbread for the daughter, she awoke her husband to find one of his cards.

The great friendliness of the three, the frank descriptions of Europe by the daughter, the brag about Chicago by the father, and the general volubility of the mother constituted the best treatment for Gilbert's depression that could possibly have been devised.

"Well, *I* reckon that Cologne Cathedral's one of the biggest frauds ever arranged on this earth. Why, we was munching something, Mar and me, and I was jest lookin' through the opera-glasses at the altar up at the end, and talking to Mar, when a beadle kind of feller he come up and——"

"You travel the hull distance, sir, *from* New York to 'Frisco in the most per—fect comfort that you cain possibly imagine. You have on board the car a library and a barber and a bath, and I cain't tell you what you don't have. Yes, *sir!* And there's no fuss nor nothin' 'bout your baggage, you onderstand me. When you leave the ho—tel you jest go to the ho—tel clerk, and you say, 'Mister, I want you——'"

"And we've enjoyed the six months purfectly. Purfectly. It's been a well-managed tower,—I will say that for Larry,—and it's learned us things that we'd no idea of before, and we've picked up bargains in Parrus that 'll simply make some of the old back numbers—friends of Julie's —turn magenta color. And if you ever find yourself within a hundred mile of Chicargo, and you don't come to see us, why, we'll never forgive you."

Gilbert said good-by to the three at the Brussels Nord Station with genuine regret. If he had known that from Brussels to Calais he was to be alone, if he had foreseen the agony of thought that his isolation would bring to him, he would have been tempted to offer them untold gold to continue the journey with him.

It was almost a grim satisfaction to him at Calais, about midnight, to find that the Channel was rough. The sea out beyond the harbor made white little cliffs of water, that disappeared and reappeared in another place; even within the harbor there was movement. Most of the passengers went discreetly below; a few only remained on the deck of the *Empress.* One, a blue-capped, tweed-coated little figure, turned up the collar of her coat, thrust her hands deep into her pockets, and strode up to the end. She asked a French sailor for a tarpaulin, and Gilbert's heart gave a big jump as he heard her voice.

"Kittie !"

The name came as an involuntary ejaculation.

"My dear, *dear* Gilbert ! This is kind of Providence ! I brought mother over to Calais for a three days' trip, and we are just getting back. She is down below." (Kittie took his arm with her old affectionate manner.) "And why haven't you written to me, you dreadful person ? Have you been so busy getting local color—you are very brown—that you have not had time ?"

"I did write, Kittie, but you will not get the letter perhaps until you reach home. I think that I ought to tell you what I have said in it."

"If you dare tell me a single word," she cried, placing her gloved hand over his lips, "I will call the captain."

"But, Kittie——"

"Sir ! will you obey me or will you not ?"

The bell rang, the last mail bag slid down the plank, and was passed along to be buried in the deep hole amidships. The board-covering to the deep hole was placed in position; the tarpaulin covering was fixed over it. The *Empress* bumped the Calais landing-stage once, as though it were playing a children's touched-you-last game, and steamed slowly out into the perturbed Channel. The lights held by the men on the landing stage waved; the sailors on board hurried below in search of early victims to *mal de mer*, and then suddenly the skies opened. The rain, pent up for hours, came down exultantly, battering the Channel, lightening the heaviness of the atmosphere; amusing with its enterprise the tweed-coated little woman standing under cover on deck in a place where she and Gilbert could stand only by pressing closely to each other.

"This is simply perfect," cried Kittie Reade delightedly. "Doesn't it make you feel very happy, Gilbert? You are a good sailor, I know."

"I'm a good sailor," confessed Gilbert, "but I am beginning to think that I am rather a bad man."

"*Farceur!*" cried Kittie. "Tell me whom you met at Coblentz."

Gilbert gave the information without details of further circumstances.

"And you did not run off with Mrs. Brentford, or marry her?"

Gilbert said gravely that his answer to the honorable member must be "No" to each of these questions.

"I'm glad you haven't enjoyed yourself much," said Kittie, hugging his arm a little tighter. "London was hideous without you. That's why I persuaded mamma——"

"Who is, I hope, quite well?"

"She is lying quite still down below with a dictionary tied round her waist, and she begged me on no account to come near her, or to say a word to her, until we reached Dover. If I hadn't met you, dear, I should have been lonely. As it is——"

"I wonder whether we shall either of us ever be really happy," remarked Gilbert.

"Good gracious!" she cried, "I had no idea that Germany had that effect on one. I don't like your change of air, sir."

"I must get you to forgive me, Kittie. I am not quite sure that I know what I am talking about."

"Go a little further," she said encouragingly; "there's a capital opening for a flattering remark. You should add that the sight of me has turned your head."

"I didn't think of that."

"This is a hard world," complained Kittie, looking out at the sea. The *Empress* seemed undecided on the respective merits of pitch and toss, and was for the present doing both. "You not only have to make compliments yourself, but you have to suggest them to other people."

"If you knew all, you wouldn't——"

The *Empress* gave a tremendous pitch into the irritated sea. A voice, belonging to a drenched lady below, screamed. The *Empress* righted herself, and proceeded penitently for some minutes in a demure manner.

"I think I ought to tell you, Kittie, exactly what is happening. And yet, somehow, I haven't the courage to."

A wave came spraying across the deck, and the two moved well back.

"I like the scent of the sea, don't you, Gilbert? There's something so—so honest about it. I say 'honest' because it is the trait that I most admire. I think, dear, that your straightforwardness and your honesty make me like you even more than——"

"The rain is stopping," said Gilbert hurriedly; "let's go out on deck."

"I declare," cried Kittie, with a tone of comic annoyance, "that I'll never say any thing nice to you again."

"I am afraid," said Gilbert, under his breath, "that you never will."

The *Empress* ran across from Calais to Dover in just over an hour and a half. Dover at 2 o'clock A. M. is not overflowing with gayety, and white-faced passengers, emerging from below after a tempestuous voyage, find little in the sleeping harbor and the misty castle on the white cliffs to cheer them. Mrs. Reade, quite buoyant at having escaped illness, was facetious at the expense of yellow-visaged travellers, glad to see Gilbert, and declared then, with one of her sudden changes of manner, that she did hope she'd never be silly enough again to go journeying about in trains, or on boats, and what not at *her* time of life. Gilbert saw the versatile old lady and Kittie into a "ladies' compartment," and found for himself a smoking.

At Charing Cross, in the gray, early morning, he hailed a four-wheeler, controlled by a fiery-faced cabman.

"What a good fellow you are!" said Kittie appreciatively. "It makes all the difference in the world to have you near to one. Is it too early to get a newspaper? I have not seen one for three days, and I always get an idea, when I am absent from London, that the worst is happening."

"I don't think I'd trouble about a newspaper, Kittie; you'll want to sleep as soon as you get home."

"Oh, dear, no, sir; oh, no! I shall change and set to work at once. Come up to-morrow morning, and let us have a good long walk in Regent's Park and listen to the discontented lecturers up near the Zoo."

"I am not quite sure where I shall be to-morrow. And, Kittie!"

She stood with one foot on the step of the four-wheeler. Mrs. Reade within had half closed her eyes.

("It don't matter," grumbled the fiery-faced cabman to himself—"it don't matter what time o' day it is, young couples must always take a 'ell of a time a-saying goo'-by.")

"Kittie, I am afraid—I am afraid something rather serious is about to happen. I want you, whatever happens, to think as well as you can of me."

"I'll do my best," said Kittie Reade, laughing.

"And you will find a letter from me at home—a letter that I wrote from Coblentz. I want you to destroy that letter without reading it."

("Nah, then," muttered the fiery-faced cabman impatiently, "*nah*, then! Are we going to wite 'ere *all* this year?")

"I shouldn't think of doing so," said Kittie decidedly. "If you have been more affectionate in that letter than you meant to be, I'll allow a slight discount; but I shall certainly read it."

"You shall *not* read it!" cried Gilbert excitedly. "I insist——"

"I wouldn't miss seeing the contents of that letter now," she said firmly, "for all the rest of the years of my life. And try to come up tomorrow morning, Gilbert. You have been away from town for so many centuries."

("'Urry up, 'urry up, there!" said the red-faced cabman; "'ave the argument out elsewhere. This ain't a debitin' society; this is a four-wheel keb.")

Gilbert pressed her hand, and Kittie looked up at him as young ladies do who expect to be kissed; but Gilbert only stepped back and raised his hat.

("Thenk Gawd!" said the cabman piously. "I shall be 'ome at the stibles before domesd'y now, if I try.")

Gilbert remained near Queen Eleanor's statue until the four-wheeler, with a small handkerchief fluttering at the window, went out of the gates into the empty, half-awake Strand. Then he took his portmanteau and walked up by Covent Garden Market, with its perfume of Kent and its crowded, cabbage-leaved pavements, to Doughty Street. He half-stumbled upstairs to his rooms, and, falling into the easy chair, went instantly to sleep.

"Well, I dever!" exclaimed Ermyntrude. The sun was staring in on the disordered youth when he awoke, with an amazement equalled by that of the small maid. "You've cub obe at last thed, Bister Gilbert?"

"I think so," said Gilbert, yawning. "But, really, Ermyntrude, I scarcely know."

"There's beed lots of callers 'ere for you, sir," said Ermyntrude, opening the window. "Very · adxious to see you they were, and just a little dasty, too, whed I told theb I diddet dow where you was. A gedlebad with a pipe id his bouth walked up ad dowd opposite for dearly all the bordig."

"That was very kind of him," remarked Gilbert.

"The bissus—*she* was quite upset over it ; she read sobethig id the papers about you, ad she got idto a rare tear over it."

"What was it, Ermyntrude ?"

"Oh, it's do use askig *be*," said the small servant; "*I* dever read the dewspapers, bless you, sir. I've got too buch to do to bother by head about what other people are doig. Do you wadt sobe hot water, sir ?"

"I should like to shave, Ermyntrude."

"You look it, sir," said Ermyntrude candidly. "I'll get you a good strog cup of tea, too; that 'll pull you together."

"I'm afraid it will take more than a cup of tea to pull me together," said Gilbert ruefully.

"Try two cups," suggested Ermyntrude.

The small maid stopped at the doorway and looked back at the mantle-piece.

"You 'aved't oped your letters, sir," she said.

The top letter was in the writing of Bradley Webbe, and Gilbert opened it first. Some of the others contained proofs; one was a fat, long envelope from a magazine.

"DEAR GILBERT:

"This will, I hope, reach you immediately upon your return from Germany. Events have been happening since your departure at an express rate, and I shall be glad when they slow down.

"Firstly, I have had my notice from the Proprietor. He had a letter before him (he said) which plainly pointed out my unfitness for the post, and he had thought it better to ask me to go at once; he would send a check in lieu of notice.

"This was rather in the nature of a whack in the eye, and I called down to see him. He declined for the present to show me the letter to which he had referred, but promised that I should see it eventually. 'He added that he was getting rather tired of the *Budget*, and he shook hands with me very warmly.

"I do not know the name of my successor. Come down to the *Budget* office as soon as you return.

"I have not yet dared to call at Regent's

Park, and under the new circumstances I cannot think of doing so.

"Yours always,

" F. Bradley Webbe."

The last letter on the pile—the pile had evidently been shuffled by the small maid—the last letter was also from Bradley Webbe.

" The Proprietor wires me that the *Budget* is to stop at once. I am preparing for next week's issue a valedictory note, and I scarcely know whether to be glad or sorry. I am certainly sorry for the man, whoever he was, who was to succeed me.

" Sincerely trust you are not affected by this Hip Hip Hurrah swindle. I know that you bought some shares in it."

CHAPTER XV

It is a notorious fact, and one known to all men, that a hand which trembles is no hand for shaving. Gilbert had all the average man's disinclination to be at the mercy of a barber for a space of minutes, and to have, in that space, soap dabbed in his eye, conversation poured into his ear, and bottles of impossible liquids for making the hair wave or cease to wave pressed upon his attention. But a man whose nerves are unstrung has no alternative.

"More weather, sir!"

"Yes," said Gilbert coldly. "It doesn't promise to be a pleasant day."

"It's what I call a muggy morning," said the youth, rubbing the soap into Gilbert's chin and looking across Holborn at a housemaid who was cleaning a window. "That's what *I* call it. Sort of morning that any thing might happen. Fond of being out o' doors, sir?"

Gilbert nodded.

"I often wish I was out 'unting, this kind of

weather," said the youth, shaving Gilbert's left cheek. "I'm a dabster on all species of outdoor sport, I am."

"Fond of following the hounds?"

"Oh," said the youth exultantly, "'ounds or any thing else. Nothing comes amiss to me. I often think to myself when I'm a-sittin' 'ere, and there's no customer, and only the old comic papers to look at, that I ought to 'ave been a country gentleman. I don't say a M. P., mind you, but—well, *you* know—jest a country gentleman. Might 'old your chin up a bit, sir."

Gilbert obeyed.

"After all," sighed the ambitious youth, wiping the razor on the small white cloth and soaping afresh—"after all, though, it's no use repining, as the song has it. We 'ave to take things as they come, don't we, sir?"

"Generally."

"And I dare say I'm as 'appy as a good many country gentlemen. In my way, of course, I mean. What you 'ave to do is to make the best of your life, whatever it 'appens to be. You shave up, on this side, I think, sir?"

Gilbert said "Yes."

"It don't do," said the youthful philosopher—

" it don't do to be too grasping. A young gentleman friend of mine—at least I call him a friend
of mine, but really I don't know his name—he
looked in this morning and had a shampoo.
He's in a solicitor's office round here in Lincoln's
Inn, and he was saying his people had got a
case on at the Mansion 'Ouse to-day over some
people that had been a bit too anxious that way."

"The Hip Hip Hurrah Mining Co."

" That's it, sir; that's it. That's the very
name. And this friend of mine was saying—
mind you, he told me this in confidence—that it
would go pretty 'ard on some of 'em, unless he
was greatly mistaken. And it all goes to prove
that what I say is right, and—a little bay rum,
sir ? No ! Pay the lady at the counter, will you,
please. Thank you, sir. *Good* morning."

Gilbert walked down Holborn into Newgate
Street in a semi-dazed condition that made the
faces of the people hurrying by appear blurred
in his sight. At any moment he might feel a
hand on his shoulder, the hand of a City detective. A City detective is *plus royaliste que le roi*—
more like a City man than any other person in
the City—but it is, nevertheless, not easy to
recognize him. The City detective comes up

17

from Brixton in the morning and hurries up to
the mysterious little office in Old Jewry with as
modest an air as though he dealt in trimmings
instead of errant men.

"Come down here."

Gilbert instinctively turned into a side passage
near him. Out in Newgate Street the yellow-
stockinged, long-gowned, leather-belted, bare-
headed boys were hurrying across from Christ's
Hospital to invest their savings in phantom food
at the confectioner's. They were all in exceedingly good spirits, these yellow-stockinged boys,
and they linked arms, and held a special meeting
in front of the confectioner's, debating the relative merits of jam puffs at three-halfpence each,
and long, empty, chocolate-looking cakes at
twopence.

"What a fool you are, Gilbert! Why the
deuce didn't you keep away?"

It was not a City detective, but Captain Dann.
Captain Dann not quite so buoyant, not quite so
affectionate in his manner of pawing; the flower
in his coat was faded and hung stem upward as
though anxious to make its escape.

"We all managed to get bail," went on Captain Dann, "but Heaven knows what is going to

happen to-day. I don't know what the Treasury
has got up its sleeve. It seems a crying shame,"
went on Captain Dann with a touch of his early
manner, "a confounded crying shame, sir, that
we rate-payers should be called upon to support
a parcel of lawyers down at Whitehall, and that
we should actually have to pay for our own prose-
cution! As I said to poor Louisa,—my wife's
very much cut up over this affair,—as I said, what
we want and what we must have some day is,
Government *by* the people, and *for* the people.
That's the way I put it. Meanwhile, we have a
lot of these what I call Tadpole and Tapers——"

" Is there—is there a warrant out against me ? "

" Oh, yes ! Yes; warrants have been granted
against all the directors."

"But, good gracious, man! *I* knew nothing of
any thing illegal being done. I was not aware——"

" Now you look here. I'm deucedly sorry
about this, and although I don't say you won't
perhaps get off, I want to give you a bit of
advice. Get away at once and stop away. If
we pull through,—the way I put it to Blenkinsop
was in a nautical way—I said it must be ' All
hands to the pump,'—why, then you can come
back. If we don't, why, you can stay away."

"I believe you are not a bad fellow, Dann."

It is an odd thing to chronicle, but it is a fact that Captain Dann's puffed eyes watered at this guarded compliment.

"And I sincerely believe you are sorry that I am in the mess. Heaven knows *I* am. It could not have come at a worse moment."

"Any moment is the worst for business like this," said Captain Dann. "The fact is, there's no chance for honest—I mean to say enterprising—men, nowadays. It's like carrying on business in a glass case. Every-body is prepared to pounce down upon you, and the public prosecutor is nearly as bad as any body else. I wonder how they expect the commerce of the empire to be carried on, eh?"

Gilbert shook his head wearily as one not desirous of arguing the point.

"Believe me, my dear sir, they'll work things up to such a pitch eventually, that it won't be worth any body's while to take a threepenny 'bus to the City. That will be the end of it. And when they've done that perhaps they will see their mistake. It's all of a piece of what I call the system of grandmotherly interference with the liberty of the subject. That's what I call it, nothing more or less."

"The fact remains," said Gilbert, "that we have to appear in the dock at the Mansion House; that we may be committed for trial at the Old Bailey, and a jury will decide——"

"Trial by jury," said Captain Dann explosively, "ought to be abolished. I've said so over and over again, but nothing has been done. I might as well have talked to a brick wall. Which way are you going? I should have shaved off my mustache, if I had been you."

"I hope your wife is well, Dann?"

Captain Dann put his hand to his eyes in an agitated way.

"Sir," he said, "that woman is a treasure. Ah! we men don't half understand how much we owe to woman." He coughed and resumed his old manner. "Indeed, my dear sir, as I often say, it is a matter of fact that when pain or—er —anguish or any thing of that kind rack the brow, why woman is, in a manner of speaking, a perfect ministering angel. But I say! What are you going to do?"

"I am going to the office, and I shall send a note to Old Jewry saying I am there, and that they have only to send a detective and I shall go at once with him——"

"I thought you had more sense than most young men. More caution. More of what our lively neighbors across the Channel call *nous*."

"So did I."

"My boy,"—Captain Dann for the first time patted Gilbert's shoulders,—"I'm disappointed in you—in a sense. In another sense I admire your pluck. For my part, I am going now to the Mansion House. Sitting begins at half-past twelve. But "—he lowered his voice—"on the steps of the Mansion House I shall be seized with a fainting fit and I shall have to be removed to my home. That will give me time to look round and to see what happens at the second hearing."

The faded flower pitched itself from Captain Dann's coat, head first on to the pavement.

"This is not the first time I've been in a hot corner," he went on hesitatingly. "The dodge is to keep your head as cool as possible. Good-by."

It was, in an odd way, a relief to Gilbert to find himself in the continuous lift at the chambers in Queen Victoria Street. The taste for being arrested on the public pavement is one not easily acquired, and it certainly seemed a more dignified act to summon the representative of the law to the office. Stepping out at the second floor and pushing the glass doors, Gilbert saw quickly that the Hip Hip Hurrah Mining Co.'s office had discarded its aspect of being extremely busy. The huge date-case on the wall was two days behind in the information that it offered; there was dust on the desk, and a jet of gas flared furiously away in the corner, where it was not wanted. One clerk only remained in the office, and he was reading the front page of the *Sporting Times* with much enjoyment.

" Is the chief clerk in, please ? "

" No," said the clerk, without looking up.

"Where is he, then?"

" Why, out," said the clerk.

The clerk laughed a little, not at his own remark, but at a paragraph in the pink journal before him.

" Is there no one here, then."

" Yes, there is."

" Who then, please."

"Why, me." The clerk looked up unwillingly. He slipped off his stool as soon as he recognized Gilbert and came toward him with a grin. "Beg pardon, sir; didn't know it was you."

"It is difficult to recognize people unless you look at them. Will you give me a sheet of note-paper, please? And an envelope."

The clerk balanced the end of a ruler on his fore-finger and kept it there with some difficulty.

"Been to Germany, haven't you, sir? There's been a rare upset here this week. Old Abbot, the chief clerk, he sloped out of it, and White and Simpson and young Congreve are out look-ing for berths, and——"

"Give me a sheet of paper at once, sir," shouted Gilbert.

"Temper!" said the clerk softly to himself as he complied with Gilbert's demand. "Temper; that's what it is. Temper and bad luck."

The letter did not take long to write. The hand-writing looked strangely unlike his usual style, as he addressed the envelope shakily:

> " *To the Superintendent,*
> " *City Police,*
> " *Old Jewry.*"

"Will you take this round at once?"

"But how can I leave the office, sir? There's no one here but me, and if——"

"I shall remain here. I shall remain here until you return with—with some one. I'll answer the telephone, if it rings."

"I shouldn't," said the clerk airily. "I let 'em ring. I know there's only an argument of some kind if I do answer it, so I just let 'em ring on. Same with callers. They've come up these last two days, and one or two of 'em that used to come up in the old times, very cocky and very haughty in their manners, I've given them beans."

The clerk chuckled at the remembrance of his successful duels.

"They get quite as good as they give me," said the clerk confidently, "now that the show's gone over. I'm on the look-out for a new berth, and as soon as I get one——"

"Please take that letter at once. I will wait here."

The clerk found his hat reluctantly, and made a cigarette to smoke on his way across the Poultry.

"More fool him," said the clerk *sotto voce*, as

he looked· at the address; "that's all I can say."

Left to himself, Gilbert took off his hat and strode round the office with hands in pockets. The marble clock on the wall ticked away conscientiously, and Gilbert knew that when it had ticked about five times sixty, a detective would arrive prepared to take him to the Mansion House. He wiped the perspiration from his forehead, and his breath came shorter as he thought of his position. Only six weeks ago he had commenced his new life with prospects so shining that they had almost dazzled him; to-day he was without a friend, without a berth, without money, and only four minutes and a half from arrest. He thought of Kittie; he thought of Bradley Webbe.

"I don't seem to have been an overpowering success," he said grimly.

He took up the clerk's *Sporting Times*, but the paragraphs detached themselves and sat momentarily on the desk, and then dodged back; all in a manner highly confusing. He took up an old copy of a financial paper, with glorious puffs of the Hip Hip Hurrah mines, and could not read that.

"In my anxiety to get on, I seem to have come off very badly. If I were to leave this life now, not a single person—nor a married person—would regret my absence. I only hope that Bradley Webbe will forgive me and that he'll—he'll marry Kittie."

Gilbert gave a big gulp, and bit his under-lip hard. But a week since, at Coblentz, the world had seemed the most delightful world that ingenuity could devise. A fortnight since he had done nothing mean; nothing of which he was ashamed. Six weeks ago he was Gilbert Staplehurst, and——

"It is of no use thinking about that," he said severely.

Yet, for almost the first time in his new life he found himself thinking of the old life that he had given up. Looking at it now, he wondered what in the world had induced him to feel the faintest shadow of discontent with his lot. He had then a charming wife, as much of fame as is good for any man, a number of friends whose faces brightened pleasantly when they saw him, he had——

"By Jove! I wish to goodness I were Gilbert Staplehurst again."

Ting—ting—ting!

"I wish I had never wanted to be young again. I wish I had never listened when——"

Ting—ting—ting!

Half mechanically Gilbert goes over to the telephone and, pressing the knob, places the tube to his ear.

"Hul—lo, there!"

"Hul—lo! Is that you?"

"Of course it is."

"Gilbert Staplehurst, I mean."

Gilbert, suddenly interested, speaks with excitement: "I was Gilbert Staplehurst once. I wish I were Gilbert Staplehurst now."

"That's what I understood from your remarks. I suppose—my name is Jove——"

"I know, I know! Go on."

"I suppose you know that it is impossible for you to return to your former existence."

"Nothing is impossible to you, Jove. I recollect in an article I wrote for the *Contemporary* about you, I mentioned that."

"I remember," says the voice at the other end. "I remember it quite well. Very good . article it was, too."

"It wasn't bad," confesses Gilbert. "If I

were only my old self again, I could do a lot of work like that."

A sound of thoughtful whistling at the other end. Gilbert, in a perfect agony of impatience, does not dare to interrupt.

"There isn't another person in the world," says the voice, "that I'd take two minutes' trouble about. But you, somehow, have always been so fair-minded——"

"I have," says Gilbert feverishly; "I have."

"——That if you're sure—if you're quite sure that you want to be Gilbert Staplehurst again——"

"I do. Indeed I do."

"It makes such a muddle in the books," complains the voice. "A lot of scratching out and carrying forward and general confusion. I really don't know that's it's worth my while to bother any more about it."

"I do hope you will. And please—*please* don't be long. I may not have an opportunity of communicating with you again for some time."

Gilbert speaks with strenuous earnestness and glances apprehensively at the ticking clock on the green wall.

"Oh, I'm not going to be in a hurry over the

matter. You have only yourself to blame for
the position that you are in——"

"I know, I know."

"And you mustn't suppose that I have nothing else to do but wait upon you. There are
other people to be considered besides you. I
have a great deal to do in one way and another,
and I scarcely know whether I am justified in
spending so much of my time on one person."

"I should never forget your great kindness,"
urges Gilbert piteously. "If there should ever
be any opportunity of taking your side in the
public press——"

"I'll make it hot for that same public press
some day, if it doesn't look out. I've seen some
most unfair, one-sided attacks upon me in it at
various times."

"Not from my pen."

"No, no, I admit that. You have always
been very impartial. If it had not been for that,
I should never have done all that I did for you."

"I wish you hadn't," muttered Gilbert.

"You think it over," says the voice. "It's
very likely that your mind is not fully made up."

"But it is. It *is* made up. And there is
really no time to lose, Jove. If you only knew

how important time was, you wouldn't hesitate a moment. Do—*do* put me back into my former life, and let every thing go on as though this had not happened."

"But how about Kittie Reade and Mrs. Brentford and Bradley Webbe, and——"

"I'm afraid," confesses Gilbert, "that they will not be sorry to lose sight of me."

The voice at the other end hums an air in a reflective, thoughtful way.

"As a special case," pleads Gilbert with much anxiety—"as a special case, you won't mind the trouble."

"What I want made perfectly clear is," says the voice deliberately, "that no one to whom you tell all this must expect to be treated in the same way. It would be a nice look-out if we had to keep on chopping and changing."

"I will particularly impress it upon them."

"And *you* won't want to change again? You won't be asking——"

"Never, never, *never*," declares Gilbert with intense excitement.

There is a sound of footsteps outside. A voice asks if this is the office, and the clerk answers that this is the shop. The clerk adds a remark to the effect that he wonders whether the young geeser is still there. The other man says that he should rather hope so.

"All right," remarks the voice at the other end of the telephone reluctantly, "but mind you, only this once."

CHAPTER XVI

GILBERT STAPLEHURST opened the door of his study in Cheyne Gardens and walked in. There was a scent of home about the room, made up of a faint suggestion of his favorite cigarettes, a more decided contribution from the box of mignonette outside the window. He sank down into his big chair and swung half round in it with a feeling of the most profound relief.

" Thank goodness ! " he exclaimed fervently.

A small Mont Blanc of white letters and cards stood on the table, and crossing his legs contentedly, Gilbert took an avalanche. The checks he stuffed into a drawer to receive attention at his leisure,—checks are a deplorable nuisance to busy literary men,—the newspaper cuttings he glanced at and tore up. Many of these referred to his brief speech at the Nomadic dinner, and some gave with the candor of the minor press those highly important details in regard to small matters that are nowadays apparently indispensable.

18

"Mr. Gilbert Staplehurst takes much care in regard to his personal appearance and is usually very correct. Why, then, he should have allowed the tape of his dress-tie to stick up at the back of his collar is one of those things that give the thoughtful pause."

And another:

"Mr. Gilbert Staplehurst is a man of many talents, but he can't orate. Still, he made a sincere, almost touching, little speech with in one place *des larmes dans la voix*, as our Paris colleagues might phrase it."

Gilbert took up the morning paper which lay folded on the side of the bookcase and looked eagerly at the date. It was quite true, then. Five minutes ago he was in the Mansion House Chambers expecting arrest and now he was—at home.

It made him pale to think how near he had been to serious disaster and how extremely fortunate he had been to have just escaped it. Really he had little to complain of. He had had an experience more novel than falls to the lot of most men, and if he could have had the satisfaction of feeling that he had done some good either to himself or to others during the last six weeks, there would have been few grounds for regret. He went to the book-case and took out his Dickens and his Thackeray,—for Gilbert Staplehurst belonged to the stalwarts,—and glanced affectionately at the volumes. It pleased him, too, to see the row of his own novels again.

"Be it ever so comfortable," he said good-temperedly, "there's no place like home."

The voice of Martha came to his ears. That excellent servant was ascending slowly the stairs, chasing the hours with shrill melody.

> " 'Roaming roaming, over the stormy sea,
> Sails my loved one, coming back 'ome to me.
> My 'eart goes out to greet him, some day I'll
> surely meet him.
> Till then my cry——' "

She suddenly stopped and called over the banisters to cook, far below. It sounded like a ventriloquial entertainment.

"Co—ok !"

"Now begin again," answered the far-off voice of cook.

"What 'll you bet the guv'nor don't come home before mistress?"

"What 'll I bet?"

"Yes, what 'll you bet. They've both been away six weeks and mistress is due this evening, and I shouldn't wonder if the guv'nor hadn't arranged so's to be home just about the same time."

Cook, below, took a few minutes to consider the wager.

"I shouldn't mind betting," called out cook, "but I always lose."

"Well," said Martha argumentatively, "some one must lose."

"Yes," said the voice of cook, "but it needn't always be *me*. How long do you reckon before mistress 'll be 'ere?"

"Not more than a quarter of an hour, perhaps less."

"Well, I've got work to do," cried cook; "it won't do for me to stand here shouting to you all the blessed day long."

"But touching this bet?" urged Martha persistently, "what d' you say? Let's have a little bit of a flutter. Make it threepence or three pennyworth of ribbon—or something."

"I'll lay you," said the far-away voice of

sportive cook—"I'll lay you a bottle of that
New Mown 'Ay scent that the grocer sells, that
mistress is 'ome first."

"Done with you," cried Martha approvingly;
"and the one that loses has to pay."

Martha took up her song conscientiously at
the point she had left it :

> " '—must always be
> Remember me, darling Jim.
> For its roaming, roaming over the——'

"I beg pardon. I *beg* your pardon, sir. I had
no idea you was here. I didn't hear you come in."

"Didn't you?" said Gilbert. He was reading
a telegram from his wife, handed in at Southampton.

"I wonder I didn't hear the hall-door shut,"
remarked Martha curiously. "As a rule I'm
very quick of hearing. The page boy has gone
out, sir. He's learning a bicycle, and he comes
home from the Embankment not fit to be seen."

"There has been no letter from Mrs. Staplehurst?"

"No, sir. Cook had a telegraph message the
same time as yours came, telling her what to do,
and cook nearly danced with joy when it arrived.
It's been a bit lonely here all to ourselves."

"I'll see that you are well paid."

"Thank you, sir. I'm sure, if it hadn't been for Arthur knocking himself about so over his bicycle, we shouldn't have had any thing to pass the time away. He's a caution, that lad. Me and cook have looked out in the papers to see if we could find where you were got to, sir, but none of them seemed to say."

"Perhaps they did not know."

"There isn't much the newspapers miss, sir," replied Martha confidently. "The evening papers especially. They do get hold of some startlers. Did you take a portmanteau with you, sir?"

"No, Martha."

"I thought not," said Martha triumphantly. "That makes another twopence I've won from—— Beg your pardon, sir?"

"Mrs. Staplehurst will be here in a few minutes, if the train keeps its time. Will you and cook see about something to eat?"

"With pleasure, sir. I hope you've had a nice time while you've been away, sir?"

"It's been—er—a little mixed, Martha. Many people called?"

"A fair number, sir. The cards are there, on

the silver tray. I told them all that you had gone abroad. Was that right, sir?"

"Yes. I—I've been abroad."

"We've been almost expecting, sir, if you'll excuse me for saying so, that you would have dropped us a line."

"Well," said Gilbert pleasantly, "I was quite sure that the house was perfectly safe with you and with cook."

Martha went down stairs flushed with the compliment which she was to halve with cook; intent also on collecting the wagers. In the hall the bell rang, followed by a quick little rat-tat at the brass knocker.

"Ah, Martha! I'm back again."

"*So* pleased to see you, ma'am."

"Every thing gone on well?"

"Yes, every thing, ma'am. Master is upstairs in his study, and——"

Mrs. Staplehurst went quickly up the thickly carpeted stairs.

In less time than might have been imagined she was kissing her husband and he was kissing her.

"My dear, *dear* Gilbert! It has seemed like years since we said good-by to each other at Paddington."

"It seems a good long while to me, dear."

"And you have been away, I hope? You're looking so well. The change has done you good, I can see."

"It certainly has done me," acknowledged Gilbert, "a lot of good."

"You must tell me all about it."

"I would rather listen to you, Alice. Has the voyage improved your mother's health?"

"She is so much better, Gilbert. And you know I didn't want to go at first, but now that it's over I'm glad I went. It's pleasant to feel that one has performed a good action, and has done something valuable for other people. Isn't it?"

"I think it must be, dear. I am afraid, though, I have had no personal experience of that during the past six weeks. I've been entirely selfish."

"And it has answered well?"

"My dear madam," said Gilbert comically; he took her chin, and looked down into her good, brown eyes, "I will not deceive you. It has failed utterly."

"Good!" cried his wife. "I dare say you wanted to write to me," she went on vivaciously, "but of course it wasn't possible. We just had two days at Cape Town and then caught the *Scot* back. If only you had been there——"

"I almost wish I had, dear."

"Still, you have managed, I expect, to get some—what is it you call it?—some 'copy.' You generally do, wherever you go. What shall you write about it?"

She looked up admiringly at her husband, and stroked his short beard.

"I'm afraid," said Gilbert thoughtfully, "that even if I were to write about it, folk might say that it didn't sound true."

"I'm very much mistaken in you, sir, if you don't make it of some use."

"I think—I think it is sure to prove of use to me."

"You met some nice people, I hope."

"I met," said Gilbert guardedly, "some exceedingly pleasant people."

"And I am sure they were very pleased to meet you. Weren't they all sorry to say good-by?"

"I don't remember any case of wailing and teeth-gnashing for the moment, dear. In fact I can't help thinking that they were all a little relieved to miss me. It's difficult to say for certain, of course, but I can't persuade myself that my existence was absolutely indispensable to any of them."

"It is to me, Gilbert."

He bowed with an assumption of great courtliness. She laughed and courtesied low.

"It's very absurd for staid, middle-aged people like ourselves," she said, "to be still complimenting each other."

"It's a habit, Alice, that grows on one sometimes. And when the wife is so delightful, and——"

"I must go upstairs and change," said Mrs. Staplehurst quaintly.

"Stay just one moment, dear. I think I never before realized how happily I was situated. I think that I see now how much I have to be—to be thankful for."

"If you are not very careful," said his wife warningly, "you will pay me another compliment."

"I declare," said Gilbert, "that I could say nothing more kind to you, dear, than you deserve. And I want you to believe that I'm very glad to be home again, and to be with you, and to——"

"I thought before I left, Gilbert," said his wife, taking off her bonnet and preparing to go upstairs to her dressing-room, "that you were becoming—becoming *un peu mécontent.*"

"I am not to be beaten by a mere wife," said Mr. Staplehurst genially, "in the use of a foreign tongue. I beg, therefore, to state (also in the language of France) that I have arrived by experience at this conclusion: *Si on n'a ce qu' l'on aime, il faut aimer ce qu' l'on a.*"

"Not a bad quotation, that."

The gong sounded down stairs; Mrs. Staple-hurst hurried away to her room.

"It is one," said Gilbert Staplehurst, "that I shall try to remember."

THE END.

www.ingramcontent.com/pod-product-compliance
Lightning Source LLC
Chambersburg PA
CBHW030626030726
47497CB00006B/1646